Topaz

Takes a Break

D1079877

WE SPARKLE WHATEVER THE OCCASION

Read all about Topaz's first year
at Precious Gems:

First term: Topaz Steals the Show
Second term: Topaz Takes a Chance
Third term: Topaz in the Limelight

And Topaz's second year:

First term: Topaz on Ice
Second term: Topaz Takes the Stage

More titles from Hodder Children's Books:

Thora
Gillian Johnson

Otto and the Flying Twins
Otto and the Bird Charmers
Charlotte Haptie

Topaz
Takes a Break

HELEN BAILEY

Illustrated by Bill Dare

Hodder
Children's
Books

A division of Hodder Headline Limited

A Catalogue record for this book is available from the British Library

ISBN 0 340 91733 4

Typeset in Baskerville by Avon DataSet Ltd,
Bidford on Avon, Warwickshire

Printed and bound in Great Britain by
Bookmarque Ltd, Croydon, Surrey

The paper and board used in this paperback by Hodder Children's Books
are natural recyclable products made from wood grown in sustainable forests.
The manufacturing processes conform to the environmental regulations
of the country of origin.

Hodder Children's Books
a division of Hodder Headline Limited
338 Euston Road
London NW1 3BH

For Lucy Drury.

A Southern Belle!

Chapter One

Topaz peered through a gap in the crimson velvet curtains and felt her stomach do a somersault. The school hall at Precious Gems was filling up with parents and teachers, all waiting for the performance to begin. She saw her mum, Lola, shake hands with the Headmistress, Miss Adelaide Diamond, before taking a seat in the front row. A man with bright red hair and thick-rimmed glasses glanced around the hall and sat down next to her. There was no mistaking him as Rodney Ruddle, Ruby's father. Dotted around the edge of the hall were trestle tables, each marked with a teacher's name. Topaz thought of her mother approaching one of the teachers to ask how she was doing at school and her stomach flipped over again.

'I don't think I can do this, I'm too nervous,' she whispered to Sapphire, who was peering over her shoulder, scanning the audience for her mother. International television and film star, Vanessa Stratton, had *promised* Sapphire she would be back from filming her latest series in time for parents' evening, but so far, there was no sign of her.

'That's not like you,' replied Sapphire. 'I thought you'd be *dying* for the curtain to go up.'

Topaz shuddered. 'It's not the curtain going up that worries me,' she said. 'It's what happens when it comes down and Mum starts talking to the teachers.'

Her mum worked as a cleaner *and* did shifts at Happy Al's Café just to keep Topaz at stage school. Her scholarship paid for the school fees, but not for the uniform, the ballet-shoes, the tap-shoes, the leotards and all the other bits and pieces that had made Topaz's first year at Precious Gems so expensive. Miss Diamond hadn't confirmed whether Topaz was to be awarded a scholarship for a second year, but without it, she would have to go to her local school, Starbridge High.

'Mum's not coming,' said Sapphire, her voice flat with disappointment. 'I knew she wouldn't.'

'There's still time,' said Topaz, knowing how hurt Sapphire would be if her mother didn't turn up. 'You said she'd promised.'

'Her promises mean nothing!' said Sapphire. 'Come on, let's go.'

Topaz let the curtain drop, and they walked back into the wings where Ruby was standing chewing the end of one of her plaits.

'You all right, Rubes?' asked Topaz. Her friend looked so pale, even her freckles seemed to have disappeared. She was to accompany the class on the piano, but a year at Precious Gems had done nothing to help conquer her crippling stage fright.

'I'm *so* nervous,' said Ruby, her voice trembling. 'What if my hands freeze on the keys or my knees knock or I suddenly can't read the music because one of the lenses in my glasses falls out or . . . ?'

'You'll be fine,' said Sapphire, giving Ruby a little hug. 'You always are when you start playing. Stop worrying!'

Ruby didn't look convinced and stuffed a thick red plait back into her mouth.

Anton Graphite, the Dance Choreographer, bustled into the wings, followed by Gloria Gold. Gloria, the Director of Music, was in a flap.

'If I could have had just a little more time to prepare them, Anton,' she twittered through pursed lips. 'Not *all* of the first years have strong voices and I really don't want my musical arrangement to let your choreography down.'

Anton rolled his eyes in despair. 'Oh for goodness' sake, Glo, get a grip!' he snapped. 'It's a group of first years performing for their parents, not a full-scale opera! The worst that could happen would be for a couple of them to sing out of key.'

Gloria gave a nervous little smile. 'You're so right, Anton,' she cooed. 'So right.'

Anton Graphite clapped his hands. 'Check you have your top hats, your canes, and take your positions!'

Nineteen pairs of black tap-shoe-clad feet tippity-tapped into a line in the wings, followed by Ruby clutching her sheet music in one hand and her stomach with the other.

Anton addressed the chorus line in a hushed voice. 'Remember, this is a class performance. No solos! No stars! No stealing the show! To your parents, you are *all* stars.' He shot a look towards Topaz, who had been disappointed there wasn't the opportunity for a solo. 'This may only be parents' evening, but remember the school motto, "We Sparkle Whatever the Occasion"!'

The chattering from the audience on the other side of the curtain died down, and the class heard a round of applause as Miss Adelaide Diamond took to the stage. Anton Graphite gestured 'Smile!' with his hands, and the class fixed wide grins across their faces.

'A warm welcome to all the parents of our first

years,' Miss Diamond boomed. 'For many of you this will be an unusual parents' evening. As you know, Precious Gems places as much emphasis on academic work as it does on the performing arts, so for parents' evening in this final term of the first year, we like to combine the two. The class will be performing the opening sequence to that well-known musical *Top Hat & Tails*, after which there will be an opportunity for you to discuss the progress of your son or daughter with each teacher.'

Topaz felt sick hearing the words 'progress' and 'teacher'.

'Enjoy the show!'

Miss Diamond nodded towards the wings. As she walked off the stage the curtain rose and, to more applause, the first years of Precious Gems Stage School filed on to the stage in purple tailcoats and black bow ties, twirling their silver-tipped canes and doffing black satin top hats. They stood in a perfect straight line waiting for Gloria Gold to give them the signal to start. But Gloria was standing at the edge of the stage, her eyes wide as saucers. The class were ready to begin, the audience were sitting expectantly in their seats, but where was the pianist? Ruby was supposed to follow the line-up on to the stage and sit at the piano, but the piano seat was empty.

The class stood like statues, grins stretched across their faces, wondering what on earth was going on. The audience began to fidget nervously in their seats, aware that *something* had gone wrong, but not quite sure what.

Topaz looked across the rows of seats. She saw her mum looking proud but confused. Rodney Ruddle was looking anxious, trying to see what had happened to his daughter. The geography teacher, Bob 'Fusty' Feldspar, was sitting at the end of a row, scowling, his arms tightly folded across his chest and his corduroy-clad legs crossed.

Bet he can't wait to tell tales about me, thought Topaz glumly, in spite of the grin stretched across her face.

The bulgy-eyed double-chinned science teacher, Trudi Tuffstone, was there too. Last term she'd told Topaz she was a troublemaker.

It wasn't my fault the classroom caught fire, Topaz thought, *but I bet old Toadstone won't say that to Mum.*

Adelaide Diamond strode back on to the stage.

'I'm afraid our pianist seems to have become lost somewhere between the wings and the stage, but our Director of Music, Gloria Gold, will step in and accompany the first years.'

Gloria looked flustered, partly because she could see Anton Graphite in the wings, slapping his forehead in despair, but particularly because Ruby had disappeared with the sheet music and Gloria didn't know the piece off by heart. How embarrassing if she gave a poor performance!

Just as she began to make her way to the piano, the door to the school hall creaked open and a pale and sweating Ruby Ruddle stood framed in the doorway.

'Ah, Ruby!' called out a relieved Miss Diamond. '*There* you are!'

Ruby looked towards the stage with cold fear. *Nothing* had helped her conquer her stage fright. Even Topaz's recent attempts to cure her with hypnosis had ended in disaster. Her stomach had been knotted all day and she'd needed a last-minute dash to the toilet, only to find, when she'd returned, that the stage door was shut. By the time she'd run round the outside of the school, up the steps, through the front door, along the corridor and into the school hall, her classmates were already on stage. Everyone was waiting for her. Everyone was staring at her.

Topaz, Sapphire and the rest of the class watched as Ruby walked to the stage with wobbly legs and uneven steps. The sheet music she clutched in her sweaty hands quivered as if blowing in a breeze.

As she passed each row of the audience, the sound of muffled laughter grew louder and louder, until a ripple of giggles spread across the entire school hall.

That's so *mean*, thought Topaz, as she noticed even her mum trying to stifle a smile behind her hands. *It's not Ruby's fault she's so nervous.*

But as Ruby climbed the steps, walked on to the stage, and turned to sit at the piano, the class saw what the audience was laughing at. Ruby had walked through the audience with the back of her grey school skirt tucked into her knickers!

Topaz and Sapphire had the same thought. They couldn't let their friend sit at the piano with her large navy-clad bottom on show, but if someone pointed it out, Ruby would bolt off the stage and out of the school hall. She might never perform again. *Something* had to be done!

Topaz moved out of the line-up, twirled her cane and tippity-tapped her way over to the piano where she stood behind Ruby, blocking the audience's view of her friend's bottom. Ruby turned to see Topaz behind her and felt a wave of relief. She didn't know why Topaz had moved out of the chorus line, but she was very pleased that she had. She didn't feel so nervous when Topaz performed next to her.

'Take it away, Ruby!' cried Topaz, doffing her top hat towards the audience.

The hall was filled with the sound of music and dancing and singing as the class performed their routine. The spotlight over the piano also illuminated Topaz, who occasionally changed the steps the class had practised, adding her own little twirls and shimmies, though always remaining close to Ruby. She was enjoying every minute of the performance, unaware that her classmates in the line-up were furious that Topaz had got herself into the spotlight *again*. Although their faces were smiling, their eyes were shooting daggers at her, particularly when she was the first to take a bow at the end and, gesturing towards her classmates, invited them to do the same.

'Who does she think she is?' hissed Jasper Pretty through his fixed grin, as Topaz stepped forward to take yet another bow. As the audience rose to give the class a standing ovation, Topaz noticed Bob Feldspar remained seated.

I don't care! she thought, lapping up the applause.

'Encore! Encore!' a few overexcited parents called out. Gloria and Anton, now flushed with success, nodded from the wings and the class began to re-form the chorus line. But barely had Ruby turned back to the piano when the door of the school hall burst open and in a whirlwind of cream satin and diamonds, Sapphire's mother entered the school hall and glided to the front like a model on a catwalk. The applause

Topaz had been enjoying dwindled away until only her mother was left clapping.

'So sorry I'm a teeny bit late!' announced Vanessa to the astonished audience. 'My private plane was late touching down. Have I missed anything?'

Chapter Two

'I can't believe my mother did that!' growled Sapphire, throwing down her top hat and cane. 'I'm *so* sorry. Why does she always have to make an entrance?'

'No worries,' said Topaz, who *was* worried, but about the fact that her mum had just left Fusty Feldspar's table with a grim look on her face, and was now heading towards Miss Tuffstone.

'I can't believe that I made an entrance with my bum on show!' wailed Ruby. 'It's not even as if I had my best knickers on! That's it! I'm never going to perform again.'

'It's not the end of the world, Rubes,' said Topaz. 'You played really well. No one will remember your knickers after the holidays.'

Ruby groaned. 'Don't remind me about the holidays. This day's been bad enough already.'

'I thought *I* was the only one who wasn't looking forward to the break,' said Sapphire as she watched her mother make her way through the crowd of parents, stopping to give her autograph to fathers, whilst mothers stared at the size of her diamonds.

'But won't you be going somewhere hot and exotic?' asked Topaz.

Sapphire nodded. 'A private villa abroad,' she sighed, 'where Mum will drink champagne cocktails all night, and sleep and sunbathe all day. It will be *sooo* boring.'

Topaz didn't think it sounded boring at all. Her mum hadn't mentioned anything about a holiday, but even if they did manage to get away, the most they could afford would be a couple of days in a caravan at Boddington Sands.

'At least you're going somewhere warm and dry!' grumbled Ruby as her father approached. '*We're* visiting a damp bog. Again.'

'Did someone mention damp?' asked Ruby's father excitedly.

'I was just telling them that because of your job we always go on holiday to damp places.' Ruby pulled a face. 'Never anywhere nice and hot like normal people.'

'*Always* damp?' asked Sapphire. 'Why?'

'Slugs,' said Ruby rolling her eyes. 'Dad studies the slithering pattern of slugs.'

Everyone gave a little gasp. Ruby always just said that her father did 'something in science'. She'd never mentioned slugs!

'I'm Professor of Limacology at Sutton and Starbridge University,' explained Ruby's father. 'A limacologist studies slugs.'

'You go on holiday with slugs?' asked Topaz, both fascinated and horrified by the thought.

'Ah, not just any old slugs,' said Professor Ruddle proudly. 'The famous rare Bolascan silver-backed speckled slug. Once a year it does a mating dance in a damp cave. It's amazing. Limacologists from all over the world come to watch. We have our family holiday at the same time.'

'You get excited over a slug?' asked Topaz incredulously.

'Well, it does dance,' said Ruby, slightly defensively.

'And you stay in a damp cave?' asked Sapphire.

'Of course not!' laughed Ruby's father. 'What sort of a family do you think we are? We stay in a tent, in a field, *next* to the cave.'

Vanessa Stratton appeared beside Sapphire. She looked annoyed.

'I'm not happy, darling,' she said. 'Not happy at all.'

Sapphire's heart leapt. Miss Diamond knew that she didn't really want to be at stage school and follow her mother into show business. What she *really* wanted to be was a scientist or a doctor, but her mother wouldn't hear of it. Perhaps Miss Diamond had said she wasn't suited to stage school.

'I'm sorry, Mum,' said Sapphire, 'but it can't have come as a shock. I *have* told you and Dad.'

'You never mentioned it,' snapped Vanessa. 'And if I'd known, I'd have made alternative arrangements. I feel very let down, Sapphire.'

'But I *told* you I didn't want to go to stage school,' persisted Sapphire. 'I don't want to be a star like you.'

Vanessa frowned. 'Darling, what *are* you talking about?'

'The fact that I would rather be a doctor than an actress,' said Sapphire. 'What are *you* talking about?'

'The fact that the caterers have obviously let the school down,' her mother replied. 'There's no

14

champagne and no canapés, and I was told that this was a catered soirée. It's just not good enough.'

Sapphire glared at her mother. 'Mum! This is a parents' evening, not a cocktail party!'

Rupert, Vanessa's assistant, was hovering nearby.

'I told her there would be champagne,' he whispered to Sapphire. 'It was the only way I could get her here.'

'So what *did* Miss Diamond say about me?' Sapphire asked her mother.

Vanessa shrugged her shoulders and began to walk away. 'Someone round here must have a spare bottle of something.'

Lola sat nervously in front of Miss Diamond. Even though she was here to talk about Topaz, sitting in front of the Headmistress brought back memories of her own school days. She had always been in trouble for daydreaming rather than working. Even now she was grown up, the feeling of dread was still the same.

Lola hadn't felt so bad until some of the teachers had begun to tell her that Topaz didn't seem interested in schoolwork. The science teacher was unhappy with Topaz, and the geography teacher had said some very mean things about her.

Lola was shocked. Until now, she'd been proud of how Topaz was doing at school. She'd even organized a surprise for her daughter as a treat for working so hard. She'd thought Topaz had been doing well. She certainly gave the impression that she took stage school very seriously. She'd done extra classes after school and on Saturday mornings, just to catch up with the others who had done stage work before they went to Precious Gems. But several teachers were very unhappy with Topaz.

'Miss Diamond, how is Topaz doing at school?' Lola asked. 'Some of the teachers don't seem very happy with her work.'

Adelaide Diamond studied Topaz's mother. She looked like an older, more tired Topaz, her brow knitted with worry. The Headmistress's large chest rose and fell, and the string of amber beads around her neck clacked gently together. She *had* planned to tell Lola that Topaz had huge potential as a performer, but made no effort with her schoolwork. She *was* going to tell her that Topaz's scholarship was still under discussion and that some of the teachers were urging her not to offer Topaz a second year. She *should* say that Topaz seemed to always attract trouble.

She sat back in her chair and looked towards the stage where Topaz had just sung and danced under the spotlight. The performance was still fresh in her mind and reminded her of the first time she had seen

Topaz at the auditions. Off stage there was nothing special or remarkable about the girl, but there was no doubt that on it, Topaz lit up the stage and captured the attention and imagination of the audience.

Adelaide Diamond leant across the trestle table and looked straight at Lola.

'Between you and me,' she said, 'your daughter could be a *big* star.'

'Miss Diamond is obviously very pleased with you,' said Lola.

'She is?' said Topaz in amazement. She'd been watching her mother talking to the Headmistress out of the corner of her eye, but hadn't been able to tell how things were going.

'She is!' said Lola. 'She said some very nice things about you.'

'Are you sure she didn't think you were someone else's mum?' asked Topaz suspiciously.

Sapphire and Ruby stared at their feet and tried not to giggle.

Lola laughed. 'Of course not! Why should she?'

'Oh, no reason,' said Topaz, still amazed that Miss Diamond hadn't told her mum about all the times she had been in trouble.

Lola put her arm around her daughter. 'I haven't said anything about a holiday this year because I was going to keep it as a surprise, but I think now is the time to tell you. I'm so proud of you that as a treat I've booked a holiday at Whoosh Waterworld when term finishes next week.'

'You lucky thing!' gasped Sapphire.

'That is *so* cool!' said Ruby.

A holiday at a water theme park was better than any sun-soaked foreign villa, and *certainly* better than slug-spotting in a damp field.

Topaz did a delighted little tap-dance and gave her mum a kiss.

'That's brilliant, Mum. That's just *so* great!'

'Why all the excitement?' said Vanessa Stratton, returning empty handed. 'Have the caterers arrived?'

'Topaz is going to Whoosh Waterworld!' said Sapphire. 'Isn't she lucky?'

'Who's Topaz?' asked Vanessa. 'And what on earth is Whoosh Waterwonder?'

Sapphire was furious. Not only had her mother been the *only* parent to arrive late, she'd wrecked the encore and now didn't recognize Topaz, even though she'd met her several times.

18

'It's Waterworld, *not* Waterwonder, and *this* is Topaz,' Sapphire snapped, pointing at Topaz who was disappointed that Vanessa hadn't recognized her. 'She's one of my best friends.' A look of sadness crossed her face. 'I wish *I* was going there instead of lying on a beach waiting for you to sleep off all the cocktails you've drunk.'

Everyone looked embarrassed at Sapphire's outburst, except Vanessa, who was beginning to think of a cunning plan. Much as she loved her daughter she really didn't want her hanging around all day, counting the number of champagne cocktails she was drinking, or nagging her about sleeping in. How perfect if she could palm Sapphire off on this other family, if only for a few days.

Vanessa turned to Topaz's mother. 'Isn't it sweet that our daughters seem to be such good friends?' she purred, flashing Lola her most charming smile. 'It's so important for girls to have friends, isn't it?'

Lola nodded. 'Changing schools is always difficult. I'm delighted that Topaz has made such good friends. Sapphire and Ruby are lovely girls.'

'Excellent!' said Vanessa. 'Then you won't mind if Sapphire joins you at this Whoosh place.'

'Mum!' shrieked Sapphire, startled. 'You can't just invite me on someone else's holiday! How embarrassing!'

Lola patted Sapphire on the arm. Even though she was a little shocked by the way Sapphire spoke to her mother, she didn't like the off-hand way Vanessa treated her daughter either.

'It's all right, Sapphire. We'd have loved to have invited you – wouldn't we, Topaz? – but I've only booked a chalet for two people.'

Vanessa was undeterred.

'Oh, that's not a problem,' she said airily. 'I'll get Rupert to arrange a larger chalet.' She nodded towards Rupert who nodded back. 'That's sorted then!'

Lola looked stunned. Vanessa looked pleased. Sapphire and Topaz beamed at each other. Then they noticed Ruby's crestfallen face. Whilst they were whooping it up at Waterworld, Ruby would be camping in a damp field waiting for the Bolascan silver-backed speckled slug to do whatever it was supposed to do.

'Will there be room for Ruby?' asked Topaz hesitatingly. The extra shifts at Happy Al's Café might pay for Topaz and her mum, but she wasn't sure whether they could stretch to Ruby.

'Of course!' said Vanessa, completely ignoring the open-mouthed Lola. 'I'll arrange for you to stay at the biggest and best chalet this Whoosh Waterwotsit place can offer.'

Professor Ruddle coughed. 'Well, I'm not . . .'

'Pleeeaase, Dad!' pleaded Ruby. 'I really really don't want to see a slug on holiday this year.'

Rodney Ruddle scratched his head. He'd never understand his daughter. She was a talented musician, yet still couldn't perform in front of an audience on her own. The Headmistress had told him that Ruby hadn't made as much progress as she had hoped, and he had told her that if Ruby was to stay at Precious Gems there had to be an improvement in the second year. And now she didn't want to go on holiday to the annual slugfest! All the top limacologists would be there, but she would rather go to a theme park! *Strange girl*, he thought, but he agreed she could go.

'Leave everything to me!' said Vanessa triumphantly.

Topaz, Ruby and Sapphire hugged each other. This was going to be the best summer holiday they had ever had.

Chapter Three

'Topaz L' Amour!' a voice bellowed. 'Why aren't you in class?'

Bob Feldspar towered over Topaz, glaring.

'I'm on my way to see Miss Diamond, Mr Feldspar,' she said, staring up at the geography teacher. 'She's asked to see me.'

Bob Feldspar curled his top lip into a tight sarcastic smile. 'Now why doesn't that surprise me?' he sneered. 'What have you done this time?'

'I don't think I've done anything wrong,' replied Topaz. 'I'm going for my end of term interview.'

Bob Feldspar looked annoyed. He liked nothing more than hearing that Topaz was in trouble.

'Well then, what are you doing standing here wasting

my time *and* yours?' he barked. 'Don't keep the Headmistress waiting!'

I can't win! thought Topaz as she carried on down the corridor.

As she approached Miss Diamond's study, a weedy boy with long eyelashes was leaving, clutching a brown envelope. Jasper Pretty looked pleased with himself.

'Miss D says I've done so well this year, I'm to be put forward for professional parts next term,' he crowed. 'She doesn't say that to everybody.'

Topaz wanted to wipe the smug smile off Jasper's face by saying, *I've already done professional parts!* but as she'd done most of them without the school knowing, even though it was against school rules, she didn't dare. Jasper was *just* the sort of boy who would tell tales on her. He still hadn't forgiven her for her solo at parents' evening.

'You're next,' he said. 'Good luck. You'll need it!'

He sauntered down the corridor sniggering whilst Topaz made faces behind his back.

Topaz peered round the door of Miss Diamond's study.

Outside in the corridor with its line of hard chairs, notice-boards on the walls and the ever-present smell of stinky school dinners, there was no doubt you were in a school. But stepping inside Miss Diamond's study was like stepping inside the dressing room of a movie star.

Soft pink lights framed a huge glass mirror fixed to one wall. Behind Miss Diamond's desk, a large glass cabinet groaned with trophies of every shape and size, five Golden Nugget Awards standing proudly at the front, next to the Golden Whisk Topaz and Ruby had won on a game show in their first term. The walls were filled with posters, press cuttings, reviews and photographs from the days when Adelaide Diamond was a huge star of stage and screen, the only actress ever to win five Golden Nuggets.

'Ah, Topaz!' Miss Diamond smiled and beckoned her in. 'Come and sit down.'

Topaz was relieved to see that the large overstuffed red velvet sofa which usually stood in front of Miss Diamond's desk had been moved to one side, and in its place were two small leather armchairs. The sofa may have looked comfortable, but Topaz knew from experience that underneath the plush red velvet lurked lumpy springs waiting to pinch your bottom and go *Ping!* for no reason. The sofa had always made her feel uncomfortable. Thank goodness for new chairs!

She sat down on one of the leather armchairs, but as she did so, it sounded as if she had sat on a whoopee cushion. She shuffled slightly on the chair and there was another deep burp. How embarrassing! It was enough to be worrying about what Miss Diamond was going to say.

'How do you think you've done this year, Topaz?' Miss Diamond asked, sitting back in her chair and running her hands through her wiry grey hair.

Topaz shrugged. 'OK, I suppose. I mean, some good bits and some bad bits.'

Miss Diamond raised a quizzical eyebrow.

'Some *very* bad bits,' Topaz admitted. 'But mostly good bits. I think.'

The Headmistress appeared troubled. 'Looking at this it seems to me that the bad bits, as you call them, are mainly to do with academic lessons.' She tapped a brown envelope in front of her. Topaz's school report! 'There are some very poor comments in here. You just don't seem interested in learning.'

'Oh I am, Miss Diamond,' said Topaz earnestly. 'It's just, I still don't see how geography or science is going to help me become a star. I love acting classes and dance classes and . . .'

The Headmistress held up her hand to interrupt. 'Topaz. Being at Precious Gems is about stage work *and* schoolwork. We *know* you can dance and sing, but if that's all you want to do, you're at the wrong school. Rhapsody's Theatre Academy might suit you better.'

Topaz shuddered. Her arch rival Octavia Quaver was a pupil at Rhapsody's. The girls there were real stage-school brats. Very brash, very confident, and very loud. There was no way she wanted to go to *any* school that had Octavia as a pupil. The thought of going to Starbridge High and having to sit near school bully Kylie Slate was bad enough, but the thought of sitting next to Octavia Quaver and her miserable friend Melody Sharp was even worse.

'But I love it here!' pleaded Topaz. 'I don't want to leave!'

Miss Diamond leant forward, her large chest smothering Topaz's school report. 'Then, if I am to renew your scholarship, you really have to start showing more application in *all* classes, not just the ones you enjoy. I can't keep helping you, Topaz, if you don't help yourself.'

Topaz nodded. 'I will, Miss Diamond, I promise I won't let you down. I've learnt a lot this year. Really I have.'

The Headmistress sat back in her chair. 'Let's start on the first day of the new term when you return after the summer holidays. I usually choose one of the older students, but I'd like you to be a chaperone for the new pupils.'

To be a chaperone was quite an honour. Topaz

remembered Pearl Wong being a chaperone when she first started at Precious Gems.

'Thank you, Miss Diamond!' said Topaz. 'I won't let you down, I promise!'

'So you've said, Topaz, but don't let yourself down either.' Miss Diamond handed Topaz her school report. 'Make sure you give this to your mother. Now off you go and remember to come in bright and early on the first day of next term.'

Topaz went to get off the chair and it gave another embarrassing burp.

I don't care! she thought. *I've got another year at stage school!*

She stopped at the door and turned back to look at Miss Diamond.

'Thank you for giving me another year at Precious Gems,' she said. 'It means *everything* to me.'

Miss Diamond shook her head. 'Topaz, I haven't. As I've written in your report, let's take it term by term.' She took another report off the pile of brown envelopes beside her. 'Term by term.'

Topaz sat in Happy Al's Café and stared forlornly at the brown envelope in front of her. She'd only been given another term at Precious Gems! What would happen after that? Even juggling two jobs, she knew her mum couldn't afford for her to stay at Precious

Gems without a scholarship. Then she'd have to go to Starbridge High. Kylie Slate's sneers and her old best friend Janice Stone feeling sorry for her would be more than she could bear. She could hear Kylie's taunting voice in her head. *Stage school reject! Stage school reject!*

Next term I'm really going to buckle down, she thought to herself. *I can't risk losing my scholarship.*

But what was she going to do about her school report? If it was as bad as Miss Diamond seemed to indicate, her mum would be devastated. Why hadn't Miss D said those things at parents' evening? Her mum had arranged a surprise holiday because she was proud of her. Now what? Would she cancel the trip, even though Ruby and Sapphire were coming too?

There was nothing for it but to find out what was in the report.

Happy Al came over to her table.

'You ordering, or just taking up space?' he said miserably.

'Has Mum got another shift today?' Topaz asked.

Al shook his head. 'She did the lunchtime rush. She's gone off to one of her cleaning jobs.'

'Then I'll have a mug of very very hot water please.'

Al reappeared with a steaming mug.

'I'll still have to charge you for it,' he said, banging the mug down on the red and white checked tablecloth. 'It takes power to heat water and power isn't free.'

Topaz held the envelope over the hot water, but instead of the seal gently opening as she had hoped, the envelope just got soggier and soggier.

Al looked over.

'You trying to steam that open?' he asked.

'Umm . . .' Topaz didn't know what to say. Al might tell her mum what she was trying to do.

'Because if you are, bring it over here.'

Topaz approached the counter with the sodden envelope. Al took it from her, held it in a pair of kitchen tongs, and, turning to his pride and joy, the state-of-the-art chrome Turbo Frother cappuccino machine, he angled the multi-directional froth nozzle and turbo steam jet towards the envelope. With a gurgle and a whoosh, steam shot out of the nozzle. He handed back the envelope, still soggy, but now open.

Topaz sat back at the table and stared in horror at the teachers' comments.

Fusty Feldspar had written: *Having taught Topaz geography for a year, I am sorry to say that she can still hardly find her way to the classroom, let alone identify any continents.*

Trudi Tuffstone said: *Topaz cannot be trusted in a science laboratory* or *to hand her homework in on time.*

The maths teacher wrote: *If Topaz spent as much time*

29

doing maths as she does practising her autograph, she would be a genius.

The history teacher had simply put: *I'm wasting my time.*

Anton Graphite and Gloria Gold had been grudging in their praise of Topaz, although they said that whilst she had talent and worked hard in their lessons: *Trouble is never far from Topaz.*

She read Miss Diamond's summary: *There is no doubt that Topaz has the potential to be a talented performer. But a career in the performing arts relies on luck as well as talent, and to build a strong career can take time. It is for this reason that the school places so much emphasis on academic lessons and Topaz must apply herself to the academic side of her education if her scholarship is to continue. I suggest that we review Topaz's progress at the end of the next term.*

Topaz sat and stared at the report. It was far worse than she had imagined. What was she going to do now?

'Bad news?' Al called out from behind the counter.

Topaz nodded.

He came over and sat down at the table.

'What's the problem this time?' he asked. 'You in trouble again?'

Topaz pushed her school report towards him. 'The Headmistress says I'm not doing well in proper lessons like maths and stuff.'

Al flicked through the report and snorted. 'They've told you that before. You've told me that before. So why haven't you changed?'

Topaz shrugged. 'If I'm going to be a star then what use is maths or chemistry? Instead of science I could be singing. It's just a waste of time.'

'You're really sure you're going to be famous, aren't you? You've really got no idea!' Al sounded bitter.

Topaz bristled. Just because Al had once been a TV star but now ran a café didn't mean the same thing was going to happen to her! After Al's prime-time TV show was cancelled, he hadn't worked in show business for years, although he'd been asked back to play Inspector Barry 'Nosey' Parker in the Christmas special of *Murder Mile* Topaz had been in.

Al read her mind.

'Don't be so sure you won't end up on the checkout at The Bargain Basket or serving burgers in Speedy Snax,' he growled. 'Talent isn't everything. Luck's just as important. Show business isn't just about talent, but about what the audience wants. Sometimes an audience knows *nothing*.' He spat the words out. 'They can't see talent right in front of their noses! Why do you think they cancelled my TV show?'

Because International Speed Tiddlywinks *got more viewers*, thought Topaz, but said, 'That's what Miss D has written. About luck, I mean.'

'That old show business bird should know,' said Al, getting up from the chair and picking up Topaz's mug. 'You should listen to her.'

'Perhaps they'll commission another series of *Murder Mile* when the TV special comes out,' said Topaz.

'Not with my luck,' replied Al, turning his back and furiously polishing the chrome on his Turbo Frother.

Topaz gathered up the report, stuffed it into her schoolbag, and walked out into the street. She'd been planning to go into town to buy a couple of tops for her holiday, but what was the point of buying holiday clothes if you might have to stay at home?

There's no harm in looking, she thought as she jumped on a bus and headed into town.

Topaz wandered around Cosmic Clobber, picking out a few T-shirts and slinging some jeans over her arm, but her heart wasn't even in browsing. As she looked at the clothes, all she could think about was how disappointed her mum would be when she saw the report. Perhaps she'd been right after all and Miss D *had* thought Lola was someone else's mother. Topaz felt that she'd got the holiday by dishonest means. Her mum had booked it because she'd thought she was doing well at school, and the report quite clearly showed that she wasn't.

'Oh come on, it'll be a laugh. So what if we don't

intend to buy them!' A sneery voice could be heard approaching.

Oh no! thought Topaz. *Not her! Not now!* She darted backwards and hid in the middle of a rack of pink pyjamas, as Kylie Slate sauntered past, chewing gum, followed by Janice Stone carrying an armful of clothes. Kylie grabbed the clothes off Janice and marched into a fitting room, followed by an assistant shrieking, 'No more than four garments in the changing rooms at any one time!'

Kylie launched a pile of clothes out of the changing room and they landed on Janice's head.

'Get me this in yellow, Jan!' Kylie put her head out of the curtain and Topaz buried herself further in the pyjamas.

'There she is! I can see her feet sticking out the bottom. The pyjamas are rustling!'

The pyjamas parted and she was faced with a furious shop assistant and a very large man wearing a brown uniform and a peaked cap marked 'Security'.

'Come out of there, young lady!' said the security guard, as Topaz emerged clutching the tops and jeans she had been holding when she'd dived in. 'Now, what do you think you are doing?'

It looked bad, hiding in a rack of pink pyjamas with an armful of clothes.

'I was hiding,' said Topaz. 'From friends. Sort of friends.'

'Hiding from sort of friends?' said the security guard sarcastically. 'That's one I haven't heard before!'

'It's true!' said Topaz. 'Honestly! One was a friend and could still be if she wasn't friendly with the one that could never be a friend because she's a bully.'

'Stop babbling and make up your mind!' snapped the shop assistant. 'You can't even get your story straight. Let's take you to the office and phone your parents.'

'She's not lying. It's true.' Janice Stone appeared beside them. 'We *were* friends and Kylie *is* a bully. Most people avoid her. She's been horrible to Topaz since she went to stage school instead of Starbridge High.' Janice smiled at Topaz. 'Topaz wouldn't steal anything.'

'I wouldn't!' agreed Topaz. 'I don't even like these!' She thrust the clothes towards the security guard.

The security guard and the shop assistant looked at Topaz, looked at Janice, and then heard a screech coming from the changing rooms.

'Get over here, Jan! I want more clothes.'

'That's Kylie,' said Topaz. 'See what we mean?'

'You,' said the security guard, pointing at Topaz. 'I

suggest *you* go home and keep out of trouble. And *you* . . .' he nodded towards Janice, '*you* might think of ditching that so-called friend of yours.'

Janice said nothing but walked with Topaz to the door.

'Thanks for sticking up for me, Jan,' said Topaz. 'It was good of you. It's nice to see you.'

'No probs,' said Janice, keeping one eye nervously on the changing room. 'How's things at the fancy school? You got any more adverts or TV things lined up?'

'I'm in the Christmas special of *Murder Mile*,' said Topaz. 'I play two sisters and one of them is dead!'

'Sounds a bit weird to me,' said Janice. 'But I'm glad you're doing well.'

Topaz pulled a face and patted her schoolbag. 'I've got a bad school report though.'

'Nothing changes then!' said Janice laughing, but looking anxiously around to make sure Kylie was still in the changing room.

'I'm a bit worried about this one,' admitted Topaz. 'Mum won't be happy when she reads it.'

'So?' said Janice. 'Do what we always did. Leave the report in your schoolbag until next term, by which time everything will be forgotten!'

Chapter Four

The last few days of term were quiet, with most of the older pupils having left for summer seasons in shows, now that their exams had finished. The moment school ended, Topaz put her uniform in her wardrobe, stuffed the horrible second-hand boy's blazer she'd been forced to wear all year – even though it was the wrong colour – under her bed, and put her school report in the bottom of her bag and to the back of her mind.

There wasn't long between the end of school and the start of the holiday at Whoosh Waterworld, and the days before they left were a wild frenzy of planning, packing and yet more packing. Topaz couldn't decide what to take, so decided to take *everything*. At the time, taking everything seemed like a good idea, but now, as

 she dragged a suitcase and two large bags down the stairs from their top-floor flat at 14 Andromeda Road, even *she* began to wonder if she'd packed too many things.

'How long are you going for, Miss Topaz?' Parks, Vanessa Stratton's chauffeur, asked as he loaded her bags into the car.

'Five nights,' replied Topaz.

'It looks as if you've packed for five months,' said Parks. 'They're heavy too. What *have* you got in them?'

'Just things,' said Topaz with a shrug. 'Things I might need.'

Lola got into the front seat and turned to Sapphire. 'Did your mum get a booking confirmation from Waterworld?' she asked. 'I haven't had anything since Rupert called to check the details.'

'I've haven't got anything,' said Sapphire with a sinking feeling in the pit of her stomach. She'd been worried from the moment her mother had taken over the booking of a larger chalet. Vanessa Stratton was well known for making grand gestures and promises she couldn't keep, especially when it came to arrangements involving Sapphire. But Sapphire had checked with Rupert and he had assured her that he had made the booking. Still, Sapphire felt uneasy.

'Never mind!' said Lola. 'They've probably got everything on computer and don't bother with bits of paper nowadays.'

Parks stopped outside Starbridge Central Station and unloaded their bags. All around them, cars, taxis and buses were pulling up, spilling luggage and excited passengers on to the pavement.

The station was packed with holidaymakers, and Lola was relieved that she'd thought ahead and made seat reservations. Vanessa Stratton had been so generous in offering to pay for a large chalet *and* getting her chauffeur to run them to the station, she thought it only right that she paid for their train tickets. She glanced up at the departures board and called out over her shoulder, 'Platform seven for the fourteen-forty to Boddington Buffers! Ruby! Sapphire! Stay with me!'

Lola led the girls through the crowds, jostling with suitcases, stumbling over children in pushchairs and dodging groups of foreign schoolchildren all wearing the same brightly coloured rucksacks on their backs.

At platform seven stood the Starbridge Flyer, its doors open, ready to welcome passengers eager to start their holiday. They found their coach, and, dumping their bags in the luggage rack at the end of the carriage, made their way to their seats. But when they sat down, someone was missing.

'Where's Topaz?' asked Ruby.

'She was behind me when we left Parks,' replied Sapphire, looking up and down the carriage, hoping that Topaz would appear at any moment.

Lola felt terrible. She'd been so busy worrying about getting Topaz's friends safely on board, she'd *completely* forgotten to look out for her own daughter. That was the sort of thing Vanessa Stratton did!

'We'd better all get off the train until we find her,' said Lola, hoping that the girls wouldn't detect the rising panic in her voice. 'Let's take our luggage too. We can't have it going on holiday without us!'

They got off the train and stood on the platform looking over the heads of the passengers hurrying towards them, hoping to see Topaz. But there was no sign of her.

'Shall I go back and try to find her?' asked Sapphire.

Ruby shook her head. 'It's safer to stay where we are. She knows what train we're on and where we're going.'

'What *can* have happened to her?' said Lola, desperately scanning the crowds.

Sapphire pulled a silver mobile phone out of her bag and flipped it open. 'I'll ring her.'

The guard began to walk along the train, closing the doors. He saw the group standing on the platform.

'You ladies getting on?' he asked. 'I'm about to blow my whistle.'

'We're waiting for someone!' said Ruby.

'Well *you* can wait for someone but the train can't,' said the guard. 'We've got timetables to run to!'

'She's not answering her phone!' said Sapphire in despair.

Suddenly there was a little *Beep! Beep!* noise and speeding towards them was a luggage cart with a flashing orange light. Waving madly from the seat behind the driver was Topaz with her three bags of luggage.

'Hope it gets better soon!' the driver of the cart called out, as the guard threw the luggage into the carriage, pushed Lola and the girls on to the train, slammed the door behind them and blew his whistle.

'What on earth happened?' said Lola as they pushed their way through the crowded train towards their seats. 'What did he mean, "hope it gets better soon", and why are you limping?'

'Too much luggage!' said Topaz. 'I couldn't find a luggage trolley and couldn't manage three bags on my own so I pretended I'd hurt my leg so that they would take me to the train on that cart thing.'

'Well you can stop pretending now,' said Ruby slightly tartly as they scrambled into their seats.

'Welcome aboard the fourteen-forty Southern

Trains Area Rail Service to Boddington Buffers,' crackled a voice over the loudspeaker. 'Stopping at Starbridge Common, Starbridge Junction, Five Bridges, Stipwick Parkway and then fast to Boddington Buffers where this train terminates.'

'Well at least we're on the right train!' said Lola brightly, as the train pulled out of the gloomy station.

Topaz looked out of the window and watched the landscape change. The grey of the town gradually disappeared, merging into green parks where children played and dogs raced around. The rows of houses with neat gardens studded with paddling pools, swings and slides began to dwindle into countryside as the Starbridge Flyer hurtled towards the coast and Boddington Buffers. Small stations flashed by so quickly, Topaz couldn't even make out their names.

'You all look happy!'

The guard was clipping the tickets Lola had handed him.

'We're all going on our summer holiday!' said Topaz, beaming.

'Have fun!' said the guard, moving on to the next seats.

'We will!' everyone said together, before collapsing in fits of giggles.

Topaz couldn't remember a time when she had felt so happy. She had a year at Precious Gems behind her, the summer holidays in front of her, and her best friends and her mum beside her. She could forget all about scholarships, Kylie Slate and Octavia Quaver. This holiday was going to be a chance to chill out.

Another voice came over the tannoy.

'My name is Paul and I'm your chief steward on board this train. The buffet car is now open for a selection of teas, coffees, hot and cold snacks, crisps and soft drinks.'

'I think I might go and get a drink,' said Topaz. 'Would anyone else like one?'

The others shook their heads.

'Maybe later,' said Sapphire.

'Do you want us to come with you?' said Ruby, getting out of her seat to let Topaz into the aisle.

'I won't be a moment,' said Topaz.

'Make sure you come back!' said her mother, only half joking.

'I'm only going to the buffet car,' said Topaz. 'Even *I* can't get into trouble doing that!'

Although only two carriages away, the walk to the buffet car took for ever. The train was packed and anyone who didn't have a reservation was standing in the aisles or sitting on their luggage. Even the queue for the buffet car stretched out of one carriage and into the next.

'A can of cola please,' said Topaz, when finally she got to the front of the queue.

'I've just run out,' said Paul, the steward. 'But we've got those.' He nodded towards a fridge full of Slurp 'n' Burp fizzy drinks. Topaz wrinkled her nose. She'd always drunk Slurp 'n' Burp until she'd discovered Octavia Quaver was the lead burp in the Slurp 'n' Burp radio adverts. Now even her favourite flavour left a nasty taste in her mouth. Still, if that was all they had . . .

'A Blackberry Burble please,' she said, handing over her money.

'Be careful it doesn't explode when you open it,' said the steward, handing her the can. 'Those drinks are very fizzy, and being on a train shakes them up even more.'

Topaz nodded and began to make her way back to her seat. Someone was blocking the aisle trying to force a large bag into the small overhead luggage rack. As she waited to get past, she held the can away from her and pointed it slightly downwards before carefully opening it.

There was a dull *pop!*, a fizzing sound and a small trickle of purple liquid bubbled out of the hole.

Hardly an explosion, thought Topaz as she went to take

43

a swig. Suddenly, a fast train coming from the other direction shot past, buffeting the carriage this way and that. As the train jolted and jumped along the rails it sent Topaz crashing sideways into the seats, spraying Blackberry Burble everywhere.

'Arghhh!' yelled a voice.

'I'm so sorry . . .' Topaz began, as a small figure jumped up, drenched in sticky purple liquid.

'You!' the purple-coated figure shouted, tossing fizzy drink from her long blonde curls.

'You!' gasped Topaz in horror.

For standing in front of her, covered in Blackberry Burble, was none other than Octavia Quaver. Topaz hadn't seen her since Raj Singh, the director of *Murder Mile*, had ordered Octavia and her mother off the set and given Topaz Octavia's role.

'Mum!' whined Octavia. 'Look what she's done to me, Mum! She's poured drink all over me on purpose.'

A large woman with peroxide blonde hair and wearing a shiny pink tracksuit erupted from her seat and filled the aisle. She had a face like thunder. It was Octavia's mother, Pauline.

'Not you again!' she barked, jabbing a finger like a fat, uncooked sausage at Topaz. 'I'm fed up of you following my princess around. Don't you have your own life?'

The carriage fell silent. Heads began to peer

over and around seats. Topaz was about to say that she had spilt the drink by mistake and was sorry, but seeing Octavia standing there like a pouting purple alien, decided she wasn't the slightest bit sorry after all.

'I bought this drink,' said Topaz defiantly. 'Why would I waste it on *her*?'

'Get back to your seat,' roared Pauline. 'I've had just about enough of you and your games. You might want to ruin my daughter's career and now her clothes, but you are *not* about to spoil our holiday!'

Octavia smirked and tried to bat her eyelids at Topaz, but finding they were stuck together, only managed a series of wonky blinks. '*We're* going to Whoosh Waterworld and *I'm* going to win the talent contest.'

'Are you OK?' asked Lola as Topaz came back to her seat. 'We were beginning to get worried.'

'You look like you've seen a ghost,' said Sapphire.

'Worse,' said Topaz glumly, her shoulders drooping. 'A real-life ghoul and her mother.'

'The gruesome twosome!' gasped Ruby. 'Octavia Quaver and her mum are on this train?'

Topaz nodded. '*And* they're on their way to Whoosh Waterworld.'

'Is Octavia that girl who was dressed as a burger in

the Speedy Snax commercial?' asked Lola. 'The one who is at the other stage school?'

Topaz nodded and grimaced.

'Did you speak to her?' asked Sapphire.

'No,' said Topaz. 'I chucked this all over her.' She waved the sticky empty can of Blackberry Burble.

Three sets of eyebrows shot up at once.

'It was a mistake,' said Topaz. 'Not that either her or her mum thinks that. I'm going to have to spend the entire holiday avoiding them.' She sank miserably down into her seat.

Sapphire reached over and patted Topaz on the arm. 'I wouldn't worry. Whoosh Waterworld is supposed to be huge, and Mum has booked the biggest and best chalet they have. We probably won't even see them once we're there.'

'Octavia says she is going to win the talent contest,' said Topaz. 'I don't know anything about a talent contest, do you, Mum?'

'I seem to remember there was something in the brochure,' said Lola.

Topaz's eyes widened. 'And you didn't think to tell me?'

'It's just a holiday park contest,' Lola smiled. 'Surely you've had enough of performing?'

Chapter Five

Passengers poured off the train at Boddington Buffers, out of the station and into the hot sticky sunshine towards a sign that said 'Taxis & Coaches'.

Although Lola hadn't taken much notice of the talent show advertised in the brochure, she *had* remembered that there was a complimentary minibus between the station and Whoosh Waterworld. It wasn't hard to spot. It was parked outside the station painted bright blue with huge white waves crashing down the side, and the slogan: 'No Need For Sun When There's Indoor Fun!' Octavia and her mother Pauline were getting on it. Octavia no longer looked purple, but she did look very sticky and there was a whiff of blackberry juice in the air.

The driver of the minibus was standing by the doors, holding a clipboard.

'Name?' he asked, his eyes fixed to the list attached to the board.

'Stratton,' said Lola. 'The booking was made in the name of Stratton.'

'There's no Stratton on my list,' said the man with a shrug.

Sapphire's heart began to sink.

'Try Love,' said Lola. 'The original booking was made in the name of Love, but it was changed at the last moment.'

Topaz noticed Sapphire and Ruby give her a strange look when her mother gave her surname as Love. She'd never told either of them that she'd changed her name from Love to L'Amour because she thought it sounded more glamorous, and she'd got away with it so far because the girls had always referred to her mum as 'Mrs L'.

The man ran a finger up and down the list and shook his head.

'Nothing in the name of Love *or* Stratton.'

'Never mind,' said Lola. 'We know we have a reservation, so we'll just sort it out when we get there.'

The man slammed the passenger door of the minibus shut and began to climb into the driver's seat.

'What's he doing?' cried Topaz. 'He's going without us!'

'No name, no seat,' said the driver, starting the engine.

As the minibus pulled out of the car park, they noticed Octavia and Pauline Quaver sneering at them from inside the bus.

'There must be some mistake,' said Lola. 'We'll get a taxi and get the Waterworld people to pay. It's the least they can do to make up for their error.'

There were no taxis standing at the taxi rank, so Lola and the girls stood in the sweltering heat waiting for one to come along. They waited, and they waited and they waited, but nothing pulled into the station car park.

'Excuse me,' Lola called out to one of the station staff. 'Is this where you get a taxi?'

'Usually,' said the man. 'But you won't see any more today. There's a big football match on. Boddington FC are playing Starbridge United in the Speedy Snax Charity Cup. All the cabbies will be there.'

'What a start to the holiday!' cried Topaz. 'We're supposed to be going to Whoosh Waterworld but the minibus left without us.'

'Oh dear,' said the man sucking in air between his teeth. 'Oh dear, oh dear.'

'There *must* be a bus we could catch,' said Lola. 'Could you point us to the bus stop?'

The man shook his head. 'There's no public transport from the station to the Waterworld, because they provide their own buses.'

'Can we walk?' asked Ruby. 'Is it far?'

'Too far to walk in this heat and with those bags.' He nodded towards Topaz's luggage.

'We're stranded!' wailed Topaz. 'What are we going to do, Mum?'

Lola shrugged. 'I don't know, girls. Let me think for a moment.'

'Tell you what,' said the man. 'I could run you over there.'

Everyone let out a sigh of relief.

'Could you?' said Lola. 'That is *so* kind of you. Thank you *so* much.'

The man smiled. 'No problem. You'll have to wait for my shift to finish first.'

'How long will that be?' asked Topaz.

'Once the last train is through. A couple of hours or so.'

The girl in the bright pink blazer behind the reception desk looked startled when she saw four tired bedraggled figures dump their bags on the floor and lean over the counter.

'I'm sorry, we're fully booked!' she said, flashing a bright white smile. 'Would you like a brochure so that you can plan ahead for your next holiday?'

'We have a booking,' gasped Lola. 'We're booked in under the name of Stratton.'

'Oh, my apologies!' trilled the girl. 'We don't usually have guests checking in this late. Welcome to Whoosh Waterworld. My name is Poppy and I'm one of the Pinkcoats, here to make your stay special.'

Topaz stared at the Pinkcoat. It was the girl from Wellington's the Chemist in Starbridge who, last year, had given her a free sample of Peachy Pores Peel-Off Face Mask.

'Weren't you the Peachy Pores girl?' asked Topaz, remembering how the sample had peeled off most of her skin the night before the casting for the Zit Stop! advert.

Poppy smiled. 'That's right, but now I'm a Pinkcoat.' She proudly stroked the lapel of her pink jacket. From promotions girl to Pinkcoat was obviously a big step up.

'You're very late,' she said. 'All the other guests have checked in by now and are enjoying Whoosh Waterworld's hospitality.'

Lola's eyes narrowed and she leant further over the counter. 'We would have liked to have been booked in by now, but because *your* booking system didn't put *our* names on the list for the minibus, we got left behind!'

Poppy looked bewildered. 'That's very unusual,' she said, tapping away on the computer. 'Could you just clarify the spelling of the name Stratton?'

Sapphire stepped forward. 'S-T-R-A-T-T-O-N,' she said. 'Stratton.'

After a few more taps on the keyboard, Poppy nodded her head and beamed. 'Found you!' she announced.

Lola, Topaz, Ruby and Sapphire let out a sigh of relief. Any moment now they would be on their way to the biggest and best chalet Whoosh Waterworld could offer. Then their holiday could really begin.

They noticed Poppy's smile fade as she studied the computer screen.

'There *was* a booking under the name Stratton for a Premium Class Lodge with luxury en-suite facilities,' she said.

'Was?' they chorused, worried by the frown on Poppy's face.

'Was,' confirmed Poppy. 'The Stratton party made the booking but didn't pay the balance of the non-refundable deposit five days before arrival. The booking is no longer valid. That would be why your name wasn't on the list for our complimentary shuttle bus.'

Sapphire couldn't contain her anger. Not only had her mother let *her* down, she'd let *all* of them down *and* ruined the start of their holiday.

'Don't worry,' she said angrily, opening her mobile phone. 'I'll ring Rupert and get him to give you my mother's credit card details over the phone. She can pay the balance now.'

Poppy gave a thin smile. 'I'm afraid that isn't possible,' she said. 'The start of the school holidays is our busiest time of year and we never have a problem re-letting chalets where a booking has lapsed.' She gave a couple of taps on the keyboard. 'A party by the name of Quaver now has your chalet.'

Topaz sank down on to her bags and put her head in her hands.

'What about our original booking in the name of Love?' asked Lola. 'I know I paid the deposit *and* the balance. Let's use that instead.'

Poppy tapped on the keyboard.

'That booking was cancelled by a Mr R. Vanderlay. I'm afraid there is no refund on any cancellations made fewer than ten days before arrival.'

'Rupert!' said Sapphire. 'Rupert cancelled your chalet but Mum never instructed him to pay the balance of the new booking. We've lost both chalets!'

'Is there *any* room at Whoosh Waterworld?' asked Ruby, who was wondering whether it was too late to ring her father and get him to come and collect her, slugs or no slugs.

Poppy made a great fuss of tapping on her computer, staring at the screen, shaking her head and giving puzzled looks before announcing, 'You're in luck! We do have accommodation available in our Chalet Mobeel class.'

Lola couldn't remember seeing a Mobeel class chalet in the brochure and asked Poppy what it was.

'It's accommodation for the budget-conscious traveller who nevertheless wants to appreciate the full facilities that Whoosh Waterworld can offer,' Poppy trilled.

'But does it have en-suite facilities?' asked Lola. 'We don't want to be walking miles with our towels and toothbrush!'

Poppy avoided Lola's gaze and said under her breath, 'Sort of.'

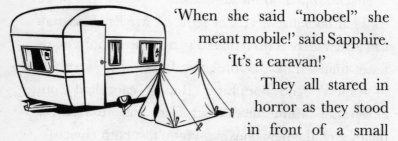

'When she said "mobeel" she meant mobile!' said Sapphire. 'It's a caravan!'

They all stared in horror as they stood in front of a small dingy-looking caravan next to a bright orange tent, pitched beside the toilet and shower block.

'Let's stay here tonight,' said Lola, opening the door of the caravan and wrinkling her nose at the musty smell coming from within. 'We'll sort out something better tomorrow morning.'

'Do you want to stay in the caravan with your mum?' asked Sapphire, peering through the flap in the tent to see two airbeds covered with sleeping bags.

'Why don't the three of us sleep in the tent and let Mum have the caravan?' said Topaz, feeling guilty that the holiday was already turning into a disaster, even though it wasn't her fault. 'I'll drag a mattress from the caravan into the tent.'

'That's settled then,' said Lola. 'Now, why don't we go and find something to eat? This place is supposed to have lots of restaurants!' She looked at the map they had been given and tried to sound brighter than she felt. 'It says that there are three restaurants. Which do you fancy trying first?'

'Whichever is nearest,' moaned Topaz, not even trying to sound bright. 'I'm tired, I'm starving and I'm fed up.'

Sapphire and Ruby felt the same, but were too polite to say so.

'What about Puddles then?' asked Lola. 'Looking at the map, it should be just around the corner.'

It was, but the door was firmly closed. Ruby peered through the glass as a Pinkcoat walked by.

'Excuse me,' called out Lola. 'Is this restaurant closed?'

'Puddles closes at 6 p.m.,' said the girl. 'It's a restaurant for our younger guests.'

Lola looked at the map again. 'What about Cascades?' she asked. 'Can we get something to eat there?'

The girl gave a bright grin. 'Of course you can. Café Cascades is by our main pool between the waterfall and the Hydro Helter-skelter, open for light refreshments from 10 until 4!'

'But it's evening!' said Lola.

'Oh, you want to eat *now*?' The Pinkcoat looked at her watch. 'The only place open now is our main restaurant, Waves, but you'll have to be quick. They'll be turning off the deep fat fryers any minute!'

Lola and the girls raced to Waves as fast as their tired legs would let them, but not fast enough. A waitress, dressed as a mermaid, met them at the door.

'I'm sorry, we've just turned off the ovens and the fryers,' she said.

'But we're desperate,' said Lola. 'You've no idea what sort of a day we've had. Don't you have *anything* to eat?'

'Take a seat,' said the mermaid. 'I'll see what I can do.'

They sat down at the nearest table and watched as the mermaid shuffled off towards the kitchens, dragging her fishy tail behind her.

Sapphire held her head in her hands. 'I'm so sorry about all this,' she said. 'It's all Mum's fault. I *knew* that something would go wrong if she was involved. I should have checked the booking myself.'

Lola patted Sapphire's arm. 'These things happen. Don't worry. Look, we're here, and we're about to have something nice to eat. Things will get better from now on! Here comes our meal now!'

The mermaid appeared with four plates of cheese on a bed of sad, limp-looking salad. 'Sorry,' she said, embarrassed. 'It's the best I could do.'

Topaz stabbed her fork into a piece of tomato, and juice and pips spurted out all over her T-shirt.

Ruby stared at her plate. 'I don't believe it,' she said. 'They're following me on holiday. Look!' She pushed her plate to the middle of the table. There, curled up in a fold of a lettuce leaf, was a shiny yellow slug.

'I'm not hungry any more,' said Topaz, throwing down her knife and fork.

'Nor me,' said Sapphire.

'Let's go to bed,' said Lola wearily. 'Things will look better tomorrow, I promise.'

The hot sticky day gave way to thundery showers. Lola lay awake in the caravan wondering if Vanessa Stratton was going to pay for any of the holiday . . . and if she didn't, just how many extra shifts at Happy Al's Café would cover it. Sapphire lay listening to the rain running down the tent, thinking that perhaps a villa in the sun with proper beds and lovely food might not have been such a bad idea after all. Ruby was sure her airbed was slowly deflating and her sleeping bag was damp, and wondered whether she was destined always to go on holiday with slugs. And Topaz? Topaz lay awake planning how she was going to win the talent contest . . .

Chapter Six

Lola was right. Things did look better the next day. The thunderstorms had cleared the air and the morning was warm and bright. After breakfast, Sapphire telephoned Rupert and told him about the cancelled booking, and Rupert said he'd make some calls and sort something out. Luckily for them, one of the other guests had broken his big toe by sticking it up the bath tap and had decided to go home, so a chalet had become available. It wasn't a Premium Class Lodge, just a standard chalet, but it was better than a musty caravan and a tent. Even better, there was no sign of Octavia or her mother.

'I told you this place was big enough for us not to run into her,' said Sapphire as they made their way to the pool. 'And even if we do, we won't let her spoil our holiday.'

The girls gasped as they entered the heart of Whoosh Waterworld – the water wonderland in a giant plastic bubble. Small pools, waterslides, fountains, waterfalls and bubbling jacuzzis surrounded an enormous shimmering blue swimming pool. Wave machines pulsed water across the pool, and cannons fired water jets high into the sky. Towering above everything was the Hydro Helter-skelter, the tallest, longest and fastest waterslide in the world.

'That looks fun!' said Topaz as they settled themselves on sun loungers and watched as every few seconds, someone came hurtling down the water-filled corkscrew slide before being catapulted laughing and spluttering into the swimming pool.

'It looks too hectic for me!' said Lola, putting on her sunglasses and lying back on her sun lounger. 'I just want to spend the holiday relaxing.'

The girls spent the next few hours lazing around the pool, reading magazines, gossiping about celebrities, watching the other guests, and munching on snacks from the poolside café. It was a perfect day. Sunlight streamed through the plastic bubble and danced on the waterfalls, and Topaz lay back and stared up through the roof at the clear blue sky.

It had been a difficult year. When she'd started at

Precious Gems she was sure she would instantly become a star, but she hadn't realized that stage school meant hard work both on and off the stage. Unlike her classmates, she hadn't had any formal dancing or acting lessons before she'd auditioned for the school, and to get her up to the standard of the others, she'd had to take lessons with the dreaded PTs, the part-timers who paid for classes at Precious Gems after their own school had finished.

She'd done some professional work, mostly without Miss Diamond's permission, but still she hadn't managed to get a starring role. Perhaps if she got good reviews for her role in *Murder Mile* when it was shown at Christmas it wouldn't be long before her agent Zelma Flint would be offering her fantastic parts and people would be saying . . .

'Just who does she think she is?'

Topaz sat bolt upright. That wasn't part of her daydream!

'Look at her!'

As her eyes became used to the bright sunlight, Topaz saw Octavia Quaver standing by the side of the pool, pouting and posing. She was wearing a tiny bikini covered in glittering silver sequins, and she was already attracting plenty of attention.

'She thinks she's a model!' said Topaz. 'Don't let her see we're looking at her!'

The three friends grabbed their magazines and pretended to read, whilst secretly watching Octavia pout and pose and preen.

'I can't believe she's wearing a bikini with sequins!' said Sapphire, peering over the top of her copy of *Hot Science!*

'It's only held together by bits of string!' said Ruby, hiding behind a copy of *Keyboard Krazy!*

Topaz threw down her copy of *Snapped!*, took off her sunglasses and pulled herself off the sun lounger.

'I'm not going to spend my holiday hidden behind magazines whilst Octavia prances about. Here we are in a water wonderland and I haven't even dipped my toe in the water. I'm going to have a go on the Hydro Helter-skelter. Anyone coming?'

As Lola snoozed, the three girls picked their way through wet towels, inflatable rubber rings and fake palm trees and headed towards the helter-skelter. But Octavia was walking in the same direction.

'I don't believe it!' said Topaz, as Octavia began to climb the steps of the helter-skelter. 'She's going to go down the slide in that stringy sequinned thing!'

'Surely she isn't going to get it wet!' said Sapphire.

Octavia had no intention of getting wet, but, bored with parading by the side of the pool, had decided that to pose on top of the tower would be far more effective. There she stood in her tiny string bikini at the top of the slide, hands on hips, smirking in the sunlight.

'She'll be at the bottom before us,' shouted Topaz over her shoulder as they climbed the steps. 'We don't even need to speak to her.'

But as the girls got to the top of the ride, they heard Octavia's shrill voice ring out.

'Get lost, you little monsters!'

She was arguing with two small boys who wanted to go down the waterslide. Octavia was blocking their way.

'*You* get lost!' one of the boys snapped back. 'We want to play, and you want to pose!'

The top of the ride began to fill up and a queue formed behind them. Octavia was pushed forward step by step, until she teetered precariously at the edge of the slide.

'Get on with it!' someone shouted.

'Is there a problem?' called up one of the pool attendants. 'Do you need help?'

'Jump!' another holidaymaker yelled from below.

'I'm not getting this costume wet!' Octavia shrieked. 'It's from the Fin & Flipper Premium range. It's meant for pool-posing only. You can't *make* me go down the slide!'

She was wrong.

Someone at the back of the queue gave an enormous push, sending everyone stumbling forward and propelling a shrieking Octavia down the helter-skelter into the water, closely followed by the small boys, Topaz, Ruby and Sapphire.

When they bobbed back up to the surface, splashing and snorting, everyone was laughing.

'That was fun!' gasped Topaz. 'Who's up for another go?'

As they clambered out of the pool and began to hurry back to the start of the slide, they noticed Octavia still in the water. She was bobbing about and waving frantically.

'Does that girl *ever* stop trying to draw attention to herself?' said Sapphire. 'She reminds me of my mother.'

Ruby had taken her glasses off to go down the ride. 'I can't see her. What's she doing?'

'Waving at everybody,' said Topaz, giving Octavia a sarcastic wave back.

Just as they were about to climb back up the ride, there was an almighty gurgling and cranking noise and the water jets, which had been spurting water into the pool, dwindled to a trickle. The waterfall stopped falling, and the whirlpool bath became still.

An alarm sounded.

'This is an emergency announcement! Please evacuate the pool area immediately. I repeat: Please evacuate the pool area immediately!'

Everyone looked confused rather than worried and began to gather up their belongings. Only Octavia remained in the pool, trying to wrestle an inflatable lilo off a small boy.

'Give me that!' she was shouting. 'I need it.'

'She really is a monster!' said Topaz as Octavia finally ripped the lilo from the boy, who ran away from the pool, crying his eyes out.

Chapter Seven

A sign appeared in the reception area:

**The pool and water facilities are closed until
further notice due to a blockage, which has
caused damage to the filtration system.
The management apologizes for any
inconvenience caused.**

An arrow saying 'Cause of Blockage' pointed to a
pair of bikini bottoms pinned to the notice, mangled
and torn but still covered in sequins. Octavia's bikini
bottoms.

'They must have come untied when she went down
the helter-skelter!' giggled Topaz. 'No wonder she

needed to wrap herself in a lilo before getting out of the pool!'

The laughter about Octavia's bikini closing the pool soon faded when it became clear that the most advanced pool filtration system in the world couldn't cope with a pair of sequinned Fin & Flipper Premium bikini bottoms. There was only one engineer in the entire country who could repair the filter system, and he was on holiday. The pool would be closed until further notice.

'We've come to Waterworld and there's no water!' grumbled Topaz as they sat in their chalet playing Snap! with half a pack of playing cards someone had left behind. 'What are we going to do tomorrow?'

Sapphire looked at the brochure. 'There's loads to do. We can play crazy golf, go bike riding, there's a games room, trampolining, tennis, ping-pong, a spa . . .'

'Ooh, I fancy some pampering at the spa,' said Lola. 'I might book an appointment for tomorrow.'

'How about bike riding then?' asked Sapphire. 'There's a woodland bike trail we can go on.'

'Sounds great!' said Ruby enthusiastically. 'Topaz, you up for it?'

'Suppose so,' Topaz replied half-heartedly. 'What are we going to do this evening?'

'There's a family quiz tonight in the Starsplash Club,' said Lola. 'I thought we might enter.'

Topaz groaned. She couldn't see how a quiz could be fun. Answering questions sounded too much like school to her, but the others seemed keen.

'Oh, go on then,' she said. 'But I bet it'll be *really* boring.'

By the time Lola and the girls had eaten, the tables in the Starsplash Club were already full of excited holidaymakers, eager to have an evening of fun. Topaz looked around the room and wondered whether this would be the venue for the talent contest. It looked fabulous! The stage at the far end of the club was draped in a curtain of pink glittery satin. Fairy lights were strung around the room and tiny stars twinkled in the ceiling. Overhead, a giant mirrored silver glitter ball slowly turned, sending streaks of rainbow-coloured light shooting off in all directions. Pink velvet chairs were dotted around tables covered in pink and white cloths. A box with a button on it had been placed on every table.

They found a table near the stage and sat down, just as an excitable man with an orange face and pink sequinned jacket bounded on to it, manically waving a microphone.

'I'm your host with the most – Bradley Bennett – and it's a warm Whoosh Waterworld welcome to the Starsplash Club, the entertainment centre for all the family!'

The audience cheered.

'First prize in the quiz is one night's free accommodation when you book seven days or more next year.'

The audience groaned. It didn't seem much of a prize. Bradley Bennett ignored them.

'It's all in here!' he called out, pulling out a battered copy of *1000 Greatest Quiz Questions* and waving it at the audience. 'So get those buzzer fingers limbered up!'

Sapphire nudged Topaz and nodded towards the table next to them where the gruesome twosome were sitting. Octavia's hair was long and loose and falling over her face like a blonde curtain. She already had her finger on the buzzer, waiting to answer a question. Her mother, Pauline, was sitting stony-faced, clutching her handbag.

'What's with the hair?' Topaz whispered. 'It's not like her to hide!'

'I expect she's feeling embarrassed about the bikini bottom incident,' Sapphire replied. 'She must realize people know they're hers.'

'I'll ask each table a question in turn!' Bradley Bennett boomed. 'A wrong answer or no answer, and the question will be given to the floor for a chance to get a Bradley bonus point. Points mean prizes so keep your fingers on Bradley's Buzzer! Let's test them out!'

Everyone pressed the buzzer on their table and a sound like a swarm of angry wasps rang out around the Starsplash Club.

'Excellent! Then let battle commence!'

The questions began and the audience answered them with varying degrees of success. Every time there was a wrong answer, the Quavers pressed their buzzer and picked up a bonus point.

'Your friend and her mother seem to have very good general knowledge,' said Lola after the Quavers picked up yet another point.

'She's not my friend!' growled Topaz, giving her mother a stern look as Bradley Bennett turned to ask them their first question.

'It's a show business one!' Bradley announced. 'Remember, fingers on Bradley's Buzzer in case this table doesn't know the answer. Who is the only actress ever to win five Golden Nugget Awards?'

Topaz was sure she heard Octavia repeat the question. She looked over and saw her mumbling behind her curtain of hair.

'Adelaide Diamond!' Sapphire and Ruby called out.

'Three points!' cried Bradley Bennett. 'On to the next table!'

The Quavers waited anxiously for Bradley to ask them their question.

'What is the largest joint in the body?'

Pauline Quaver sat still clutching her handbag and Octavia kept her head down, hidden behind her hair, but said loudly, 'So you want to know what is the largest joint in the body?'

'That's right,' said Bradley Bennett.

Pauline and Octavia sat in stony silence.

'I'll have to hurry you!' said Bradley.

'The knee!' called out Octavia.

'Three more points!' Bradley cried.

Topaz stared at Octavia. She was sure she was up to something, but she couldn't work out what. Octavia glanced up from under her curtain of hair and saw Topaz watching her.

'What?' she sneered.

'Nothing!' said Topaz, narrowing her eyes and continuing to watch Octavia.

'Stop staring at me!' hissed Octavia.

'Or what . . . ?' Topaz hissed back.

'Or I'll tell my mum!' Octavia snorted, tossing her head to reveal an earpiece.

Topaz began to press Bradley's

Buzzer over and over again. Bradley looked confused.

'You're keen!' he said. 'This table has answered the question correctly so there are no Bradley bonus points.'

'They're cheating!' announced Topaz.

'Topaz!' gasped Lola. 'You can't say that!'

'I can,' said Topaz. She pointed at Octavia who was trying to look innocent. 'She's got an earpiece and I bet her mum has a phone in that bag!'

The audience became restless.

Pauline Quaver stood up and looked defiant. 'This is a family quiz and I'm using technology to include my family. I'm on the phone to my husband Kevin Quaver.'

The noise from the audience grew louder.

'Her husband could be on the internet at the end of the phone!' shouted someone. 'Cheat!'

Soon the Starsplash Club was ringing with chants of 'Cheat! Cheat! Cheat!'

Bradley stood stranded on the stage in his pink sequins, wondering if he had the strength to control an angry crowd with just a microphone.

'How *dare* you accuse of us cheating?' snapped Octavia. 'There's nothing in the rules to say the family has to be in the room. If anyone's breaking the rules, it's *you*. It's a family quiz and you lot aren't even family!'

'You don't know that!' snapped Topaz. 'We could be sisters!'

'What!' Octavia snorted. 'A round redhead, a blonde beanpole and . . .' she wrinkled her nose at Topaz, 'a mouse!'

'A mouse!' roared Topaz. 'Who are you calling a mouse?'

Bradley Bennett turned crimson under his orange tan. It made his face look as if it were about to explode.

'Ladies, ladies. I am sure we can sort this out.' He turned to Pauline. 'Is your husband still on the phone?'

He was.

'Then let me have a word with him.'

Pauline brought the phone to the stage and handed it to Bradley.

'Mr Quaver. Are you on the internet at the end of the phone?' he asked.

There was a pause.

'I see,' said Bradley. 'Sorry to have troubled you.'

He handed the phone back to Pauline.

'What did he say?' demanded Topaz.

'He said he wasn't on the internet,' said Bradley.

'And you believe him?' asked Topaz. 'I know these people!'

'You calling us cheats?' shrieked Pauline, her jewellery rattling with rage. 'That's slander or libel or . . .'

Octavia burst into tears. 'Mum! Don't let that horrid girl call Dad a liar!'

Bradley had a strong desire to stick his microphone

in Pauline Quaver's mouth, but smiled instead and said, 'Ladies and gentlemen, I can confirm that technically there is nothing in the rules which says that a family member has to be present in the room, so that technically Mr Quaver *could* be on the other end of the phone.'

The crowd began to boo and leave the club.

Bradley Bennett brandished his microphone in what he hoped was a menacing way. 'However!' he called out. 'That is hardly in the spirit of the game and therefore I declare this quiz abandoned!'

'But we've won!' shrieked Pauline. 'We got the highest score. We are the winners. You can't abandon the quiz when we've won!'

Topaz, Ruby, Sapphire and Lola began to leave the Starsplash Club. Octavia was leaning against the doorpost waiting for her mother to finish ranting at Bradley Bennett, who was trying to unplug his buzzers.

'We won,' she sneered as they walked past.

'Ignore her!' Lola ordered. 'Let's go back to the chalet.'

But Topaz couldn't help herself. She stopped at the door and glared at Octavia. 'Like it's a prize really worth winning!'

Octavia gave a sarcastic laugh. 'You Precious Gems girls just don't get it, do you?' she sneered. 'It's not the prize that's important. It's being a winner. Something you know *nothing* about.'

'Oh yeah?' snapped Topaz. 'Just wait until the talent night. Then you'll see who's a winner.'

'You won't win,' said Octavia. 'I'll make *sure* you don't.'

Chapter Eight

Topaz leant over the reception area where Poppy was tapping away on her keyboard.

'Good morning,' she said. 'Do you have details of the talent contest?'

Poppy stopped typing, swung round in her chair, grabbed a leaflet from a cubbyhole behind her and swung back again. She pushed it across the counter towards Topaz.

First prize was the chance of a contract with top show-business agent Zelma Flint. Topaz felt her stomach lurch. Zelma Flint was *her* agent. She might not like her, and she certainly didn't trust her, but what if Octavia won the talent contest? Would Zelma drop Topaz in favour of Octavia, and even if she didn't, could Topaz *bear* to have the same agent as Octavia?

'Are you going to enter?' asked Poppy. 'I can put your name down now if you like.'

Topaz was about to give Poppy her name when she thought of Ruby and Sapphire waiting for her in the chalet. She knew they wouldn't want to enter the contest. It still seemed strange to Topaz that both her friends were at stage school but neither of them showed the slightest interest in being a star or becoming famous.

'I'd like to think about it,' she said.

'OK!' Poppy trilled, and went back to clattering away on her keyboard.

Topaz began to walk back through the reception area to the chalet. Her mum was right. It was only a silly little talent show at a holiday park. The prize wasn't even a definite contract with Zelma Flint, only the chance of a contract. Even if Octavia won, Zelma might not take her on. She scrunched the leaflet into a ball and tossed it into the nearest litter bin.

I'm already a professional! she thought to herself. *I don't need a talent show to prove it!*

She heard a car roar up and screech to a halt. Moments later a man staggered in carrying a roll of pink net, a huge bag of silver sequins and an armful of pink feathers. Topaz recognized him as Octavia's father, Kevin Quaver.

'I'm here to deliver these to the Quaver chalet. My

daughter Octavia needs them for the talent night!' He dropped everything on the floor. 'I can't stop, I've got loads of leads to follow up in this area.' He handed Poppy a business card. 'I'm salesman of the year, three years running, for Wunda Windows Double Glazing. I could do you a very good deal in replacement windows if you're interested.'

Octavia is taking this talent night very seriously, Topaz thought to herself as she watched Poppy struggle with the net, sequins and feathers.

Topaz walked back to the litter bin and began to root around in the rubbish. She pulled out the crumpled leaflet, now stuck to a banana skin.

'I'd like to take part in the talent competition after all!' she said, marching up to Poppy. 'Please could you put my name down?'

'No way!' screeched Ruby when Topaz came back to the chalet and told them what she'd done. 'This is supposed to be a holiday!'

'You should do this, Rubes. It will be good practice

for your stage fright,' said Topaz, surprised at just how angry her friend was.

'You sound just like my dad.' Ruby flung herself on her bed.

'But we always perform well together,' pleaded Topaz. 'Remember parents' evening?'

Ruby thought of her navy knickers on show at parents' evening and slammed her face into her pillow.

'Sapphy, tell her we'd go down a storm, will you?'

Sapphire shook her head. 'I'm saying nothing and I'm *definitely* not entering. If you want to do this, you're on your own.'

'But I can't,' said Topaz. 'I've already entered us as The Gem Set. You can't have one person in a group called The Gem Set.'

Ruby sat up on her bed. She knew that the real reason she was so angry wasn't because Topaz had entered her into the talent contest, but because she was still terrified of performing. After the knicker incident at parents' evening she felt even more frightened of being on stage. So much could go wrong! But Topaz was right. This was a chance to try and get over her stage fright. No one knew her here so if she did make a mistake, what did it matter? It was only a local talent contest and there was no doubt that she felt much better on stage when Topaz was there to take the spotlight. Her dad would be pleased when she told him.

'OK,' she said. 'I'm sorry I was snappy. I'll do it. What were you thinking of performing?'

'The tap-dancing routine from *Top Hat & Tails* we did for parents' evening,' said Topaz. 'That went down well!'

'I'll need time to practise,' said Ruby, already beginning to feel nervous. 'I think I can remember the music off by heart, but I'm not sure.'

'We've got half an hour to practise in the club tomorrow,' said Topaz. 'I've already booked a slot!'

'But what about props?' asked Sapphire. 'You need a top hat and tails, a cane, some tap-shoes . . .'

Her voice trailed away as Topaz dragged one of her bags out from underneath the bed and opened it.

'I brought them all with me,' she said, flinging her purple tailcoat, black top hat, tap-shoes and silver-topped cane on the bed. 'Just in case. I'll give them back to the school next term.'

Sapphire shook her head. 'We should have guessed that's why you had more luggage than anyone else! Now, shall we go and get the bikes?'

Topaz gave her friends a sheepish look. Now that she had entered the talent contest, she *had* to make sure she won it.

'Would either of you mind if I stayed behind and practised my routine?'

Ruby groaned. 'Oh, go on then. If not, you'd just be

jiggling about on the saddle and trying to tap-dance on the pedals.'

'We'll see you later!' said Sapphire as she and Ruby headed off.

'I don't like to think of you on your own,' said Lola, who was off to treat herself to some pampering at the spa. 'Are you sure you'll be all right?'

'I'll be fine!' said Topaz. 'How much trouble can I get into hanging around the chalet?'

Topaz sat on the veranda in the sunshine and watched her mother head off to the spa. In the distance she could see Ruby and Sapphire cycle along a path until they disappeared into the forest. She was surprised to feel a stab of loneliness.

It was my decision to stay behind, she reminded herself. She had to get her song and dance routine perfect. She couldn't risk Octavia winning the contest *and* being taken on by Zelma Flint. The routine she had performed for the parents' evening was good, but it was designed for the entire class, not all of whom were confident dancers. Somehow she had to make it special.

She went back into the chalet and picked up her top hat and cane. There was no point in taking her tap-shoes since she'd just be practising her routine on the grass. Walking out on to the veranda she twirled her cane, only to see it flying out of her hand, up into the air and over the balcony, landing at the feet of a very surprised man.

'You could have taken my eye out!' The man looked up at Topaz. 'You didn't, but you could have done!'

'Sorry!' she said, scrambling down the steps and retrieving her cane. She obviously needed more practice than she'd realized.

She began to wander around, looking for somewhere suitable. The mini-football pitch was packed with boys running around with footballs; the tennis courts were busy; the crazy golf area was out of the question. People were already looking at her strangely.

I suppose a girl in shorts with a top hat and cane does look a bit odd! Topaz thought to herself as a group of girls giggled at her. *I must find somewhere no one will find me.*

Suddenly she had a thought. On the first night at the grotty Chalet Mobeel they'd had to use the communal toilet and shower block. It was long and wide, and most important of all, it would be quiet.

Perfect! Topaz thought to herself as she stood at the door. The building was badly lit and smelt of bleach and air freshener, but as she had predicted, it was empty. She began to practise her routine. The floor was hard and smooth and she wished she had brought her tap-shoes. Perhaps she would go and get them later. She spun, she twirled, she shimmied. She danced up and down the block, round the basins and in and out of the cubicles. She might be practising in a dingy toilet block, but in her head, she was on the stage, in the spotlight, moving to the music until the crowd leapt to their feet with a round of applause.

As she spun out of one of the cubicles, she clattered straight into a woman about to go in. The woman looked at Topaz suspiciously. 'What's going on?' she asked.

'Er . . . the toilet is blocked,' said Topaz, hoping the woman would leave her to practise in peace. 'They're all blocked and *really* disgusting.' She pulled a face. 'Try the ones by the pool.'

The woman left in a hurry.

Thank goodness! thought Topaz.

She danced until she felt too tired to continue and sat down on a closed toilet seat to get her breath.

I'll just nip back and get my tap-shoes, she thought. But as she was about to leave the cubicle, there were footsteps, the lights went out, a door closed, and she heard the sound of a bolt moving across a lock. There was another, lighter, pair of footsteps.

'This block has been reported out of order until further notice,' a man's voice called out. 'You'll have to use the facilities by the pool.'

There was a rustling of keys and the sound of footsteps receding into the distance.

Topaz tried the door. It was locked. She rattled the handle.

'Excuse me!' she called out. 'I'm locked in.'

There was silence.

She shouted. She whistled. She banged on the inside of the door with her cane. But no one heard her.

Now what? she thought, looking around.

At one end of the block was a row of small windows, just beyond reach.

If only I was a little bit taller, she thought, jumping up and down, trying to see out of the window.

She noticed her top hat sitting on one of the basins. It was just the right height, but if she stood on it, it would collapse. The hat would be ruined and she still wouldn't be able to see out of the window.

At first, she carried on dancing. There was no point in wasting valuable practice time feeling sorry for yourself, and someone was bound to come along soon. But as the hands on her watch went round, and round again, Topaz didn't feel quite so confident. She tried again to call for help, but still there was only silence. She leant against a basin and sighed. This was supposed to be the holiday of a lifetime but so far, *everything* had gone wrong. Not only that, but it had gone wrong for Sapphire and Ruby too. What if they went back to school next term and told the others, 'Yes, we had a great holiday, other than the few days we spent with Topaz and her mum.' How could she live that down? The teachers were right. She *did* attract trouble. She felt a tear roll down her cheek. Then another and another until she was sobbing. She glanced into the mirror and looked at her tear-stained reflection in the gloomy light.

For goodness' sake, she thought, grabbing a handful of paper towels and rubbing her face. *Get a grip and stop feeling sorry for yourself. Things have gone wrong but you're still on holiday with your friends and you've got a talent competition to win!*

She was about to throw the paper towels in the bin when she had a thought. Grabbing as many paper towels as she could, she stuffed them into her top hat. It was full, but only half full. She needed something else. Darting into one of the cubicles she grabbed the end of the toilet paper and began to pull it off the roll, stuffing it into her hat. When the roll was empty she went into the next cubicle and did the same. Eventually the hat was packed with paper.

That should help stiffen it! she thought as she put it under the window and carefully climbed on it.

CRACK! She felt the hat crumple and it sank a little but she could see out! The window was too small to squeeze through, but just large enough to lean out of.

Brilliant! thought Topaz, looking around. But her initial thrill at opening the window vanished. There was no one about. She looked at her watch. Lunchtime. Everyone would be in one of the cafés or having a packed lunch on the forest trail like Ruby and Sapphire. And where was her mum? Probably stretched out in the spa waiting for her toenails to dry, unaware that her daughter was trapped in a toilet! Topaz rested her elbows on the window ledge and waited and waited . . .

Slap . . . slap . . . slap . . . It was the unmistakable sound of someone walking towards her wearing flip-flops. *Slap . . . slap . . . slap!*

'Hello!' called out Topaz. 'Is there anyone there? I'm stuck in here!'

The flip-flops stopped slapping.

'Hello! Please! I'm up here!' she called out, waving a paper towel out of the window. 'I'm trapped in the toilets!'

The flip-flops got nearer. Topaz felt a huge wave of relief as whoever was wearing them turned the corner.

Thank goodness! she thought. *Any minute now I'll be out of here!*

The owner of the flip-flops stopped under the window and looked up at Topaz. It was Octavia Quaver.

'Oh, if only I had a camera!' Octavia gave an evil laugh. 'You look like you're in prison!'

Topaz scrunched up the paper towel and threw it down at Octavia. 'Just get me out of here,' she said. 'Please.'

'Not until you tell me how you got stuck!' said Octavia, dodging the missile.

Topaz thought about making up some fantastic story about being abducted by an alien cunningly disguised as a Pinkcoat, but lying about the toilet being blocked had got her into this mess. It was time to tell the truth, even to the gruesome Octavia.

'I came in here to practise my routine for the talent competition,' said Topaz. 'I left my tap-shoes on my bed but when I went to go and get them, I found the door was locked.'

Octavia said nothing but flip-flopped round the corner.

Slap . . . slap . . . she reappeared.

'The door has got a bolt and a padlock,' she said. 'I'll have to go and get some help,' and she shot off as fast as her flip-flops could carry her.

That's strange, thought Topaz. She had fully expected Octavia to walk off, leave her stranded, carry on laughing at her, *anything* but offer to help.

Perhaps even Octavia has a good side, mused

Topaz, twirling her cane at the thought of being released.

There was a rustle of keys, the bolt creaked across the lock and the door opened. Lola rushed in and hugged Topaz, followed by Sapphire and Ruby. A Pinkcoat was accompanied by a man wearing blue overalls carrying a tool bag.

'Thank goodness you're safe!' said Ruby, putting her arm round Topaz.

'I wish you'd come on the bike ride with us,' said Sapphire. 'Then this wouldn't have happened.'

'What did happen?' asked Lola. 'How did you get stuck?'

'I was in the toilet and then someone locked it!' said Topaz, thinking that at least that part of the story was true.

'Are you all right?' asked the Pinkcoat. 'Do you need a doctor? And why are you carrying a top hat and cane?'

Topaz shook her head. 'I'm just hungry,' she said. 'I've been in here for hours. I was practising my routine for the talent night.'

The Pinkcoat looked sternly at Lola. 'What was your daughter doing on her own for so long? We know that parents need a holiday too, but we do like them to take responsibility for their children.'

Lola looked upset. 'I'm sorry,' she said.

The Pinkcoat turned to the man in the blue overalls. 'And Bill, when one of the guests reported the toilets were blocked, didn't you check there was no one in there before you locked up?'

Bill looked flustered. 'I did, but I didn't see any closed doors so I just assumed they were empty.'

'Then you assumed wrong,' said the Pinkcoat. 'I'm not happy, Bill, not happy at all, but I won't report you to Head Office, not unless it happens again.'

Topaz felt terrible. This was all her fault. Getting stuck in the toilet wasn't just bad luck for her. It had got her mum *and* this man called Bill in trouble. Lola would blame herself for being a bad mother and not keeping an eye on Topaz, and the guilt would ruin her holiday. This wasn't just a disaster, it was a disastrophe!

A disastrophe was the worst possible level on Topaz's three-level disaster scale. The 3-D scale took into account not just the actual disaster, but the long-term consequences of the disaster. A minor annoyance was the lowest class of disaster, a disasterette. Level two was a straightforward disaster. Level three on the scale was the worst possible disaster in the worst possible context with catastrophic consequences *for life*. In other words, a full-scale disastrophe.

Suppose, for instance, you had forgotten your swimsuit when you went on holiday. This could be classed as any one of the three levels on the 3-D disaster scale. At first, leaving your swimsuit behind would be a disaster. But then, if you found a shop which had lovely swimsuits in, swimsuits which you wouldn't have even looked at if you had brought your own, then leaving your costume at home wouldn't even feature on the 3-D scale, in fact, it would have been a *good thing*. But if the shop didn't have your size so that you ended up with a swimming costume which was OK, but not perfect, that would be a disasterette. It wouldn't stop you swimming, but you wouldn't feel quite right wearing it. But if you had forgotten your swimsuit, the shop had sold out of *everything* that fitted and so you had to spend your holiday huddled under towels whilst everyone else was swimming and splashing, that was a disaster. But a disaster could quickly escalate into a disastrophe. Suppose the owner of Fin & Flipper swimwear was also on holiday and looking for a model. Whilst you huddled under a pile of towels looking miserable, Octavia would be pouting and posing in one of the many swimsuits she had brought with her and the owner of Fin & Flipper would say, 'Ah, that girl is a star! Let's use her for our next catalogue!' Leaving your swimming costume at home would turn out to be a disastrophe.

* * *

'Thank goodness for Octavia,' said Lola as they sat in Waves that evening. 'I know you girls don't like her, but she seemed very helpful. Perhaps you should give her a second chance?'

Topaz looked sullen.

'It's true,' said Ruby. 'We were sitting on the veranda wondering where you were when Octavia came rushing up telling us that you were stuck. If it wasn't for her you'd still be trapped.'

'I would have escaped somehow,' grumbled Topaz.

'But you didn't,' said Lola. 'You said you were stuck there for hours.'

Octavia rescuing her *and* getting the credit from her friends and family. If there was anything worse than a disastrophe, then this was it. A double disastrophe!

'Make sure you say thank you when you next see her,' said Lola.

Topaz pushed her chips around her plate and said nothing.

There was an awkward silence at the table until Sapphire said, 'On the bike ride we met some really nice twins who go to school in Pippersquick. One of them wants to be a scientist but her older sister can't decide between being a vet or a riding instructor.'

'But she's only older by thirty seconds!' chipped in Ruby. 'Imagine that!'

Topaz felt even more miserable and a little bit jealous. Whilst she had been stuck in the loos, Ruby and Sapphire had been off making new friends without her.

A shadow crossed the table as Pauline Quaver loomed over them.

'I gather my princess was a real star today!' she boomed. 'Octavia saved your daughter's life!'

Topaz rolled her eyes. 'Getting stuck in the toilets at a holiday park is hardly a life or death situation!' she muttered, just loud enough for everyone to hear.

Lola glared at Topaz and then smiled at Pauline Quaver. 'Thank you,' she said. 'I'm grateful that Octavia acted so quickly and came and got me. Is she around so that Topaz can thank her herself?'

Topaz shrank down in her seat and angrily speared a chip with her fork. Just when she thought the day couldn't get any worse, it looked like she was going to have to be nice to the Evil One.

Pauline Quaver rattled her jewellery. 'She'll be over for the karaoke competition, but she's at our Premium Class Lodge polishing her routine for the talent contest. She's *very* dedicated.' She looked at Topaz and pulled a sneery face. 'I don't know why anyone else is bothering to enter. Octavia is a professional and will obviously win.'

Topaz sat up straight. Octavia might have rescued her but that didn't mean that she was going to be forever grateful to her, and it *certainly* didn't mean that she was going to let Octavia win the talent contest without a fight.

Lola gave Pauline Quaver a smile which said, *I'm being nice to you because your daughter helped my daughter, but don't push it*, and said, 'Topaz and Ruby are entering. They're very good.'

Pauline snorted. 'We Quavers are used to winning. It's a shame the karaoke competition is for adults only, or Octavia would walk it, but I'll be winning it for the Quaver family. Talent! You've either got it or you haven't.'

Pauline stomped off warbling a tune out of key.

'I hope she sings better than that in the competition,' said Lola, 'or all the dogs in Boddington will be howling tonight!'

Chapter Nine

The Starsplash Club was filling up with chattering families. Bradley Bennett was bounding about the stage in his pink sequins, moving this and arranging that. At one side of the stage stood a box and a huge television screen flanked by large speakers. The karaoke machine!

Sapphire waved across the room, and two identical girls waved back.

'Who are they?' asked Topaz.

'The Pippersquick girls I was telling you about,' said Sapphire.

'They're *really* nice,' said Ruby. 'We might try and do something together tomorrow if the pool still isn't fixed.'

'Remember we've got to practise for the talent contest,' said Topaz sharply. 'It's only two nights away.'

The lights dimmed slightly, and the audience, whose chattering had been deafening, fell silent.

'Welcome to the Karaoke Song Challenge sponsored by Speedy Snax!' Bradley Bennett announced excitedly. 'This one is strictly for the grown-ups but everyone can vote!'

There was a loud cheer from the audience.

'We've got some *greaaat* prizes, so don't be shy. Now, who's going to be the first to take the Speedy Snax Song Challenge?'

'Me!' Pauline Quaver's hand shot up, as did Bradley's eyebrows.

'A *very* keen contestant. Come on up!' he called out, as Pauline rushed through the tables and towards the stage as if being chased by a herd of wild animals. Once there, she grabbed a microphone from Bradley and stood panting heavily into it.

'And tell the audience who you are,' said Bradley.

'Octavia Quaver's mother, Pauline.' She waved at Octavia who stood up and waved back.

'And what are you going to sing?' Bradley asked Pauline, who was still waving at Octavia.

'Tonight, Bradley, I'm going to sing "You Are My Everything" and dedicate it to my princess Octavia.'

Octavia, who had only just sat down, stood up and began waving again.

Topaz turned to her mum. 'You should enter this,' she whispered. 'You've got a great voice. I've heard you sing in the bath.'

Lola laughed and shook her head. 'My performing days were over the moment you were born.'

Performing days? Topaz gave her mum a sideways glance. Sometimes her mother hinted she knew more about show business than she was letting on. Could she once have been on the stage? Why didn't she talk about the days before Topaz was born, and why would she *never* answer questions about Topaz's father?

Lola noticed Topaz looking at her. One day she would tell Topaz more about her father and about her life in show business, but not yet, and certainly not on holiday at Whoosh Waterworld.

Pauline Quaver stood on the stage and looked out at the audience as Bradley loaded her song on to the karaoke machine. Any minute now the audience would be eating out of the palm of her hand. She'd always wanted to be famous. After she left school, she used to sit at the checkout at The Bargain Basket supermarket and dream of becoming a star.

She'd been dreaming of fame and fortune when Kevin Quaver had come into the shop to buy a packet of Bacteria Buster breath fresheners. He'd asked her to come outside and she'd been so impressed by the size of the custom-fitted spoiler he'd had fitted to his car, she'd agreed to go on a date with him. The next thing she knew she was getting married in a rush and then Octavia was born. How she'd have loved to be famous for something. Anything!

That's never going to happen to my princess, she thought as the song started. *She's not going to meet a man with a flash car and find her dreams shattered. I won't let her!*

At first, the audience sat in stunned silence as Pauline Quaver shrieked her way through her chosen song. Then they started to giggle with embarrassment. Pauline didn't seem to notice. She was enjoying herself. Topaz looked at Octavia, but instead of being embarrassed at her mother's high-pitched howling, she was clapping and smiling, mouthing the words to the song. There was no doubt that the Quavers supported each other.

'Pleease, Mum,' insisted Topaz. 'You'd be so much better than her.'

Lola shook her head and took another sip of her

drink. She had no intention of getting up on stage.

Finally, and much to everyone's relief, Pauline Quaver came to the end of her song, and red faced and sweating, staggered off. As she passed their table she paused and crowed, 'Talent! It's in the genes!'

After Pauline came a woman who walked off halfway through because she decided she didn't like the song after all; a man who started to sing and then realized he couldn't read the screen without his glasses; a tall, thin, sad-faced woman who burst into tears at the first chorus and fled the stage sobbing; two women who brought their drinks up with them and couldn't sing for giggling; a man who couldn't sing but told Bradley Bennett he'd come up on stage for a bet, and two brothers who had good voices but sang a duet at totally different speeds.

'Is there anyone else before we start the judging?' called out Bradley. 'Remember, we have some fabulous prizes!'

Lola looked at the stage and its shimmering pink curtain. Overhead the glitter ball sent streaks of coloured light bouncing off the walls. She remembered the days when she was in the Starbridge Follies dancing troupe, playing the lead feather in the Feather Fandango dance. How good it would feel to be up there again, in front of an audience. Lola understood when

Topaz said she felt she had to perform. The stage seemed to beckon them both. Without even realizing it, she rose from her seat and started to make her way to the front.

Topaz gasped and Ruby and Sapphire shouted, 'Go for it, Mrs L!'

'A last-minute entry!' shouted out Bradley Bennett. 'Come on up!'

Lola climbed the stairs to the stage and Bradley handed her the microphone.

'And you are?'

'I'm Lola Love,' she said a little shyly, looking bewildered under the spotlight.

'And what are you going to sing for us, Lola?' Bradley asked.

'I don't know,' she said, looking at the list of songs rolling on the screen. 'Perhaps, "Disco Meltdown" by Donna Spangle.'

Lola stood awkwardly on the stage as Bradley loaded the song on to the karaoke machine.

'You know your mum's surname is Love and yours is L'Amour,' whispered Sapphire. 'Is that because your dad was foreign or something?'

'Mum never talks about him,' replied Topaz.

The music started and Lola began to sing. She was no longer shy or awkward. It felt good to be up there on stage and took her back to the time when she wasn't a cleaner or cooking all-day breakfasts in Happy Al's Café.

'But she's changing the words!' Pauline Quaver jumped up from her table. 'It's not karaoke if you change the words!'

'It doesn't say that in the rules!' shouted back Topaz as she watched her mum singing her heart out on the stage whilst the audience clapped along to the music.

Pauline looked furious and Octavia sat glaring at the stage.

The song was over, and a blushing Lola left the stage to whoops, cheers and claps from the audience.

'You were brilliant!' said Topaz hugging her mum as she came back to the table. 'I was so proud of you.'

'Well done, Mrs L,' said Ruby. 'That was fantastic!'

Sapphire gave Lola a hug. 'The audience loved you. So did we!'

Lola took a gulp of her drink. 'Thanks, girls. It was only a bit of fun.'

Lola was the last contestant. The judging was about to start.

'As this is for fun, we're going for a show of hands!' said a beaming Bradley. 'Now, how many votes for act number one, Pauline Quaver singing "You Are My Everything"?'

Everyone looked around. No one had their hands up

other than Pauline, who was voting for herself, and Octavia who had raised both hands. Bradley, embarrassed at the lack of votes, pretended to count around the room.

'Everyone put both hands up when it comes to voting for Mum,' Topaz whispered to the others.

'And now for contestant number two . . .'

Even bad singers did well if there were enough friends and family to vote, and there was plenty of cheering and hands shooting up for most of the acts. Finally, it came to Lola.

'And last, but I think we can definitely say not least, was Lola Love singing "Disco Meltdown"!'

The crowd went wild. There was no need to resort to Octavia's trick of putting both hands up. The audience was a sea of waving arms and cheering. Topaz hugged her mum and Sapphire and Ruby hugged each other.

Bradley Bennett jumped up and down on the stage waving a pink envelope.

'Lola Love, you are the Whoosh Waterworld Speedy Snax Song Challenge Karaoke Champion. Come on up!'

Lola climbed on to the stage.

'Ladies and gentlemen! The winner!' Bradley handed Lola the envelope.

'What is it, Mum?' asked Topaz as her mother came

back to the table. 'What have you won? Is it a cheque?'

'I don't know,' said Lola.

'It might be gift tokens,' said Ruby.

'How exciting!' said Sapphire.

They all peered as Lola opened the envelope and pulled out her prize. A voucher for four free meals of Crispy Duck Dippers from Speedy Snax's Oriental range.

Chapter Ten

'We've been burgled!' gasped Ruby the next morning, as she came back to a scene of chaos inside their chalet.

Clothes had been tossed on the beds and on the floor, drawers emptied, a bed stripped of its bedding and moved, magazines strewn across every surface and bags opened, their contents scattered around the room.

'No we haven't!' Topaz scrambled out from underneath one of the beds. 'I'm just looking for my tap-shoes!'

She pushed a chair to one side. 'They're not here and I *know* I packed them.'

'When did you last see them?' asked Sapphire, following Ruby into the chalet and picking her way through the piles of belongings.

Topaz thought back. 'Yesterday morning. The day I got locked in the loos. They were on my bed and it was only when I decided to go back and get them I realized that I was locked in!'

'Well they must be here somewhere,' said Ruby. 'You don't just lose a pair of tap-shoes.'

'With red sparkly ribbons,' added Topaz. 'I left the ribbons on after parents' evening.'

'Come to think of it,' said Sapphire, 'I *do* remember seeing your tap-shoes.'

'When?' asked Topaz.

Sapphire began to pace around the room.

'We came back from the bike ride, your mum was already back and sitting on the veranda. Ruby, you were talking to Mrs L, and I came in here to get my copy of *Hot Science!* and the shoes were on the bed.'

'What happened next?' Topaz asked.

'Well, then there was all that commotion with Octavia rushing up and saying you were locked in the toilets, so I ran out and then we all scooted off to rescue you.'

Topaz's eyes widened. 'Where was Octavia?' Her head began to swim with suspicious thoughts.

'We left her here, on the veranda,' said Ruby. 'I remember looking back and seeing her.'

'Was the door to the chalet open?' Topaz asked.

Sapphire shrugged. 'I don't remember closing it.'

'Octavia has stolen my tap-shoes!' exploded Topaz. 'She must have done!'

'But why?' said Ruby. 'She must have *loads* of tap-shoes of her own.'

'To stop me winning the talent contest!' said Topaz. 'That's why! I told her my tap-shoes were on the bed. She didn't even need to look! She was at the scene of the crime *and* she had a motive. We've got to get them back.'

Ruby looked worried. 'What are you going to do? You can't just march up to their chalet and accuse Octavia of theft.'

'Why not?' said Topaz. 'We all know she's done it!'

'No,' Sapphire corrected her, 'we *think* she's done it. We don't know for sure. Remember how angry Mrs Q got when you accused her of cheating at the quiz night? We don't want a scene like that again.'

'But she *was* cheating, she admitted it, and I *know* that Octavia is the shoe thief!' Topaz kicked a magazine across the floor in frustration. 'I'm determined to prove it even if you won't help me.'

And with that, she marched out of the chalet.

The Quavers' chalet wasn't hard to find, since it was the biggest chalet at Waterworld. It was about four times the size of theirs, had a veranda going round three sides, pot plants and a full range of patio furniture.

This could have been ours, thought Topaz, creeping round the back and peering through a window. Inside, she saw Octavia kneeling on the floor, fiddling with a mound of pink net and some feathers. Her costume for the talent contest! There was a huge television in one corner, several sofas and a big table, but no sign of any shoes.

Topaz tiptoed round to the side of the chalet where there was another window, but it was frosted and she couldn't see in. Now what? Sapphire was right. She couldn't just march up to the door and accuse the Quavers of a crime when she had no proof. She leant against the side of the chalet, planning what to do next.

'Topaz!' hissed a voice. 'Come away. You'll get caught!'

She looked round to see Sapphire and Ruby standing by one of the other chalets, waving madly and beckoning her away.

'Ow!' Topaz was hit on the back of the head by the opening of the window behind her.

Pauline Quaver pushed her head through the window and looked at Topaz. She filled the entire window frame.

'You!' she snarled. 'What are you doing hanging around outside our toilet window? You got locked in a toilet a few days ago. Do you have a *thing* about toilets?'

'No!' said Topaz, rubbing the back of her head. 'I was just . . .'

'Just what?' demanded Mrs Quaver.

Topaz thought quickly. She looked straight into Pauline's eyes and said, 'I was hoping to borrow a pair of Octavia's tap-shoes as I seem to have *lost* mine. I need them for the talent night.'

Pauline Quaver's eyes narrowed. She didn't like the way Topaz said the word 'lost'.

'I could come back with my mum if you like,' Topaz added.

Topaz saw Pauline Quaver's expression change. She knew it! Pauline *did* know what had happened to her tap-shoes – and Pauline knew that she knew it!

Mrs Quaver gave a forced smile. 'Come to the front and I'll see what I can do,' she said, slamming the window.

Topaz went to the front of the chalet. She could hear raised voices inside. After a few minutes, both Pauline and Octavia appeared.

'Here,' said Octavia, 'take these. When Mum told me that you had . . . *lost* yours, I thought I might be able to help.' She handed over a plastic bag. Topaz could feel the outline of a pair of tap-shoes.

'Thank you,' she said through gritted teeth. 'I'll make sure you get them back.'

Topaz walked away from the chalet as Octavia and her mother stood watching her leave. Glancing back, she saw the gruesome twosome laughing.

She caught up with Sapphire and Ruby who had been hiding round the corner.

'What happened?' asked Ruby. 'What's in the bag?'

'A pair of tap-shoes,' said Topaz. 'They *knew* I was on to them and so, in a roundabout way, they've returned them.'

'What do you mean, in a roundabout way?' asked Sapphire.

'Well obviously they couldn't give me back *my* shoes or that would be proof they're shoe thieves, so they've given me a pair of Octavia's.'

When they got back to the chalet, Topaz opened the bag and tipped out a pair of bright red tap-shoes. She began to slip a foot into one of them.

'Ugh!' said Ruby. 'I wouldn't want to wear her shoes. Are you sure she hasn't got a verruca or something horrid?'

'It doesn't matter whether she's got galloping foot fungus,' said Topaz, angrily kicking the shoe aside.

'They're too small. I can't wear them. I *bet* they knew that when they gave them to me.'

'What are you going to do now?' asked Ruby. 'How are you going to perform a tap-dance routine without tap-shoes?'

'What on earth's been going on?' Topaz's mother walked into the chalet. 'Have we been burgled?'

'That's what we thought!' giggled Ruby. 'But it was just Topaz looking for her tap-shoes.'

'Sorry, Mum,' said Topaz. 'We're just about to clear it up. Octavia has stolen my tap-shoes. She took them off the bed when I was locked in the toilet yesterday.'

'Are you sure?' asked Lola. 'Because if you are, then I'll go over and have a word with her mother.'

Topaz didn't want her mum to get into an argument with Mrs Quaver. 'I'm pretty sure, but not totally sure. I *have* looked everywhere.'

'You'll probably find them just as we're packing up to go,' said Lola. 'It's always the way.'

'But how am I going to enter the talent contest without tap-shoes?' Topaz wailed. 'The entire act is ruined!'

Lola put her arm around her daughter. 'I've just heard the pool is going to reopen later this morning. How about we see if we can get a taxi into Boddington town centre now and find a shop that sells tap-shoes.

You'd probably need some new ones for the start of next term anyway. Then we can all come back and relax by the pool.'

Topaz jumped on the spot with delight. 'Oh Mum, thank you, thank you! We've got a rehearsal booked at the Starsplash Club later. It would be great if I could have them for that so I could break them in for the talent show.'

'Let's just get this chalet cleaned up first,' Lola said. 'It seems as if you have emptied every bag we have on to the floor.'

As she bent down to pick up a pile of papers, she noticed a long brown envelope addressed to 'Lola Love' lying on the floor. Topaz froze. It was her school report! She'd shoved it in the bottom of her bag as Janice had suggested, but in tipping everything out to look for her tap-shoes, she'd dropped the report. Now her mother was reading it, her face darkening with every page she turned.

Topaz knew she was in *big* trouble.

'Sapphire, Ruby, could you give us a moment please?' Her mother's voice was hard and cold. 'I need to have a word with Topaz. Alone.'

The girls could hardly get out of the chalet fast enough.

Lola held up the report. 'Well?' she said.

'I forgot to give it to you,' said Topaz. 'I was so

excited about the holiday I just forgot. I would have given it to you when I remembered.'

'Why was it open?' asked Lola.

Topaz shuffled uncomfortably from one foot to another. 'I guess it just sort of opened itself in my bag,' she mumbled.

She was a good actress but she couldn't fool her mother who said nothing, but stood, stony-faced, holding the report. She knew her mother would stand there all day until she got the truth.

'It's a bad report,' Topaz admitted. 'I got Al to steam it open with his Turbo Frother. I thought if you read it you'd cancel the holiday and you wouldn't be proud of me any more.'

Lola's eyes blazed. 'Of *course* I was proud of you,' she snapped. 'Even though I knew that some of the teachers weren't happy with you, I was still proud of what you'd achieved. I never thought you'd stick at doing lessons after school and on Saturdays. I thought you'd be expelled in your first term. But if I was proud of you then, I'm not proud of you now.' Lola waved the report in the air. 'Steaming it open before I'd even read it! Keeping it from me! Lying to me!'

Topaz was shocked. Her mother had never been this angry with her before. She hung her head. 'I'm sorry, Mum,' she said. 'I didn't think.'

'That's right, Topaz, you didn't think. You *never* think what consequences your actions have on others or even yourself, and it's about time you did.' Lola looked around the chaotic chalet. 'You can start by clearing up this mess.'

Topaz began to pick up the things she'd tossed around the room. 'I'll do this quickly and then we can go into Boddington,' she said.

'Oh no,' said Lola. 'We're not buying more tap-shoes now. You don't deserve them.'

'But it's not my fault Octavia stole my tap-shoes,' wailed Topaz. 'If she hadn't stolen them I'd still have them.'

'And if you hadn't lied about your school report, you'd have new ones,' retorted her mother. 'And that *is* your fault. If you still want to enter the contest that's up to you. But you'll have to do without tap-shoes.'

The girls lay on the sun loungers by the pool. Ruby had earphones on and was listening to music; Sapphire was flicking through *Hot Science!* and Lola was lying with her eyes shut feeling terrible that she had been so hard on Topaz, but not knowing what else to do to try and make her daughter more responsible. Topaz was miserable. Her mum was furious with her. Ruby and Sapphire could detect that there was an atmosphere and were embarrassed. *And* she had no tap-shoes.

She watched Octavia arrive at the pool. Pauline Quaver was trotting after her wearing an enormous shiny beach wrap and carrying an armful of towels. She looked as if she was wrapped in purple foil. They settled themselves on the other side of the pool.

'I'm going for a swim,' Topaz said as she left the sun loungers and walked to the side of the pool. She slipped into the water and began to swim up and down. The water felt good and the sound of others having fun around her lifted her spirits. She saw Octavia leave her sun lounger, walk to the side of the pool and spread her towel at the edge. She lay on it, posing, leaning on her elbow and propping her head up.

Topaz swam up to the side of the pool and leant over the edge.

'You knew those tap-shoes were too small for me, didn't you?' she said.

Octavia ignored her.

'I said, you knew those shoes were too small for me,' Topaz repeated, shouting above the noise of the pool.

'Keep away from me,' snarled Octavia. She rolled over and lay on her back.

Despite what Ruby and Sapphire had said about being careful not to accuse Octavia, Topaz couldn't help herself. She hauled herself out of the pool and stood, dripping, over Octavia.

'You know what happened to my tap-shoes, don't

you? Admit it. You were trying to stop me from winning the talent contest.'

'I said, get away from me!' snarled Octavia, sitting up and trying to pull the towel from under Topaz's wet feet. 'I don't know why you're so bothered about a pair of tap shoes, you wouldn't have won anyway!'

'Then if I wouldn't have won, why go to the bother of stealing my shoes?' snapped Topaz. 'Are you scared I might win?'

'As if!' Octavia snorted, rearranging herself on the towel and shutting her eyes.

It was no good. Octavia was never going to admit to being the shoe thief.

As Topaz walked away from Octavia she saw a sign: *No Dive Bombing.*

She looked back at Octavia stretched out beside the pool on her towel.

It was too good an opportunity to miss. She ran towards the water and, tucking herself into a tight ball, launched herself into the pool. Octavia's yells could be heard even under water.

Chapter Eleven

The girls stood on the stage and looked around the Starsplash Club. In the cold light of day it looked completely different from the fairy-lit wonderland at night, and it was difficult to imagine it filled with the sound of happy holidaymakers having fun under the twirling glitter ball. The walls were stained yellow and the carpet grubby and covered in bits of chewing gum. The pink velvet chairs looked stained and faded, and the tables, stripped of their tablecloths, were grey plastic. Some of the shades on the fairy lights were missing, others cracked and patched together with sticky tape. Dirty glasses were dotted around the room, and even the pink satin curtain across the stage looked frayed and torn.

'You'll need to get an adult to sign this,' said a Pinkcoat, handing Topaz a form and a pen.

Topaz looked at the sheet of paper. It seemed to be saying that if during the rehearsal they managed to strangle themselves in the glittery curtain or electrocute themselves on the microphone, Whoosh Waterworld accepted no responsibility.

'Can't we practise now and get my mum to sign it later?' Topaz asked. She didn't want to waste valuable practice time.

The Pinkcoat shook his head. 'Sorry girls, but it's the rules.'

'OK,' said Topaz. 'Give me a moment.'

She slipped into the wings and scribbled 'Lola Love' across the form.

'Here we are!' said Topaz, waving the form at the Pinkcoat.

'That was quick!' said Sapphire knowing full well that Topaz had signed the form instead of Lola. Once, Topaz had even forged *Sapphire's* mother's signature.

Ruby was looking round the room. 'Where's the piano?' she asked.

'We don't have a piano,' replied the Pinkcoat. 'Just an electric keyboard.'

Beads of sweat broke out across Ruby's forehead. 'I don't think I can play an electric keyboard,' she said.

The Pinkcoat laughed. 'You don't even have to play

this thing to get it to work. You can just put a computer disk in and sit at it. It plays itself! Have fun! You've got thirty minutes.' He left the stage.

Ruby still wasn't happy. 'It's not a piano,' she grumbled. 'I was expecting a piano. I *need* a piano.'

'Don't stress, Rubes,' said Topaz. 'It looks like a piano, it's got keys like a piano, just think of it as a piano with a plug!'

'But it won't sound as if it's a piano!' protested Ruby.

'Well I don't sound as if I'm tap-dancing,' said Topaz. The heel and toe movements she made in her trainers sounded as if she was sweeping the stage.

Ruby went to touch the keyboard and a loud harsh note reverberated around the room. Her stomach churned. If she was like this when the club was empty, what would she be like when it was full? She began to fiddle around with the knobs, dials and buttons. She'd never played proper keyboards before, only a little electric organ that her brother had been given for Christmas. She was surprised to discover she was enjoying herself. She found a switch which changed the sound from an organ to a piano. By twiddling some knobs, the sound changed again from a piano to a guitar. There was a string section, one for brass, woodwind instruments, and even percussion.

Whilst Ruby felt happier, Topaz was sinking further into despair. The dance number she had chosen was a tap-dance routine, but without the sound of tap-shoes, the dance would be ruined.

Sapphire, who had been sitting in the wings reading, heard a door open and close and the sound of hurried footsteps. Out of the corner of her eye she was sure she saw the curtain rustle. She looked up and was surprised to see that whilst Ruby was beaming and happily practising on the keyboards, Topaz was sitting on the stage, dangling her legs over the side, looking distraught. Sapphire went and sat next to her.

'What's up?' she asked her friend, who looked close to tears.

Topaz shrugged. 'Nothing,' she said.

Sapphire gave her a nudge. 'Well that's obviously not true!'

'I'm going to pull out of the contest,' said Topaz. 'I can't do a tap routine without tap-shoes. Let's spend our last day tomorrow by the pool and then watch Octavia win the talent contest.'

Then she burst into tears.

'This isn't like you,' said Ruby, who had stopped

playing when the sound of Topaz's sobs had drowned out the music. 'What's wrong?'

'She's going to pull out of the talent contest,' said Sapphire, 'unless we can find some tap-shoes.'

Ruby felt a rush of relief that she wasn't going to have to perform after all, even though she felt sorry for Topaz. She handed her a hanky.

'It's not just the tap-shoes or the talent show or even the Evil One,' said Topaz blowing her nose. 'It's *everything*! I wanted this holiday to be perfect, but right from the start things have gone wrong. You,' she nodded towards Sapphire, 'could have been on a sun-kissed beach with blue skies and palm trees and you,' Topaz looked at Ruby, 'could have been with your family making scientific discoveries.' More tears fell and bounced off Topaz's flushed cheeks. 'That man Bill was in trouble for locking me in and now Mum is mad at me for steaming open my report and at Happy Al for helping me. *Everything* I do turns out to be a disastrophe.'

'Stop exaggerating,' said Sapphire firmly. 'Everything you say is true, but you're forgetting something important.'

Topaz gulped and sniffed at the same time. It sounded like a loud watery snort. 'What?'

'If we'd gone on holiday with our families, we wouldn't have been on holiday with you or your mum!'

'But . . .' Topaz began.

'But nothing!' insisted Sapphire. 'I love my mum but she drives me mad. Some of the problems on this holiday have been her fault, not yours. She's unreliable, she never keeps promises, she's never there for me, she drives Dad mad which is why he's always abroad, and she always has to be the centre of attention. Your mum is lovely. She's a proper mum!'

Ruby handed Topaz another tissue. 'And I'd have been looking at slugs in a damp cave. What sort of holiday is that? It doesn't matter what happens, as long as it happens together.' She touched Topaz's hand. 'It's just a silly little talent contest at a holiday park. You don't need to prove you have talent. We know you have. You know you have. So what if Octavia wins?'

Topaz looked at her friends. 'You're right,' she said. 'It doesn't matter that I'm not going to be in the contest.' She jumped to her feet. 'I'll go and tell them to cross our names off the list.'

They all heard the noise. A whispered but high-pitched 'Yes!' coming from behind the curtain. Topaz darted towards the curtains and parted them, coming face to face with a jubilant Octavia and her mother, punching the air with delight. The moment they saw Topaz they scurried away.

'They've been spying on us!' said Topaz. 'Can you believe it?'

Ruby and Sapphire exchanged glances.

'We can't let the gruesome twosome get away with that!' cried Ruby. 'You can't let Octavia win without a fight!'

'We won't let you pull out,' said Sapphire. 'You're going to sing and dance tomorrow night whether you like it or not!'

Topaz couldn't believe what she was hearing. 'But what about my tap-shoes? How can I tap dance without tap-shoes?'

'What about another sort of dance?' suggested Sapphire. 'What did you do before you learnt to tap?'

'Nothing,' Topaz shrugged. 'Before I had tap-shoes I used to push drawing pins into my trainers to make the right sound.'

'And did it work?' asked Sapphire.

Topaz laughed. 'At the time I thought it sounded great but that was before I had the real thing!'

The three of them looked at each other. They all had the same thought.

'Right,' said Ruby. 'Let's visit every notice board in Waterworld. We've got drawing-pins to collect and a talent contest to win!'

Chapter Twelve

'And it's a warm Whoosh Waterworld welcome to the Search for a Star talent contest!' A hyperactive Bradley Bennett bounded on to the stage to wild applause. Not only did he have a pink sequinned jacket, his trousers were covered in pink sequins as well. Light danced from the revolving glitter ball and bounced off his sequinned suit, sending pink sparkles shooting in all directions. He looked like a firework. 'We've got a fabulous line-up of future stars for you tonight. Oh yes we have!'

Oh no you haven't! thought Topaz as she waited backstage, watching some of the other contestants warming up.

'First prize tonight is the chance of a contract with

Zelma Flint, one of the world's top show business agents based in that star-studded town, Starbridge! Can we have a big round of applause for Miss Zelma Flint?'

The crowd clapped and cheered, but peering from the wings, Topaz couldn't see any sign of Zelma. A plume of smoke rose from one of the tables at the front of the room.

'As this is a family entertainment centre, could I ask you please to respect our no smoking policy in the Starsplash Club,' said Bradley primly.

There was a cough, a splutter and as the smoke cleared, Topaz saw Zelma Flint. She had a cigarette in one hand and her mobile phone in the other.

'Ah, Miss Flint, there you are,' said an embarrassed Bradley.

Zelma glowered, stubbed her cigarette out on the table and, unable to smoke, began furiously sucking on the end of a pen.

'Tonight, *you* the audience are the judges, unless there is a dead heat. Then Zelma's vote will be the tie-breaker!'

The audience roared and clapped and Topaz began to worry that this audience would clap at *anything*.

'To help me on stage this evening is a particularly beautiful Bradley's Buddy. Please welcome Poppy and her Clapometer Clock.'

Poppy, in a long pink dress, appeared on stage pushing a trolley on which was perched what looked like a giant pink clock.

'Now let's test the clapometer!' shouted Bradley. 'Fire her up, Poppy!'

Poppy fiddled about around the back of the wheel, and the needle burst into life, hovering at one o'clock.

'Now if we don't like an act, what do we do?' shouted Bradley, and the audience gave a low boo.

The needle quivered but hardly moved.

'And if we quite like an act?'

The audience clapped enthusiastically and the needle moved to six o'clock.

'And if we *really* like an act?' boomed Bradley. 'How do we vote?'

The audience clapped and cheered and the needle hovered at eight o'clock.

Topaz saw Pauline Quaver at a table near the front of the stage looking smug. Topaz felt worried. Pauline had *big* hands. She could probably make a very loud noise with those hands. If she clapped really loudly for Octavia, her claps alone might send the clapometer needle flying.

'And now for the first act – Trevor the ventriloquist!'

A stocky bald man with bushy eyebrows walked on to the stage with his left arm up a shaggy yellow dog puppet. There were loud cheers from one of the tables and an attractive blonde woman shouted, 'Go for it, Trev!'

'Hello, holidaymakers!' shouted Trevor. 'Meet Shaggy the dog!'

Shaggy's mouth opened and he barked 'Woof! Woof!' The problem was, so did Trevor.

'Doesn't he realize that being a ventriloquist means that your lips aren't supposed to move?' whispered Topaz. 'He can't even bark without moving his lips.'

The acts went on and on. There were lots of acts who sang their songs out of key, forgot their words or in one case, both; a man who managed to hit himself in the mouth with his microphone, knocking out his front tooth which landed in the lap of a startled Zelma Flint; and a magician who, unable to get hold of any doves, used a pigeon instead. Unfortunately, when the bird flew out of his hat it landed on the revolving glitter ball, spraying pigeon poop into the crowd. It seemed that everyone at Whoosh Waterworld knew *someone* who thought they were talented enough to entertain an audience.

There were more boos than cheers and the clapometer needle barely moved. The audience began to get restless. This wasn't the evening they had been promised. This was a disaster. Topaz looked round the side of the stage and noticed that Pauline Quaver had left her seat and was now sitting at the keyboard, her handbag on her lap.

'I didn't know Pauline played,' said Ruby, who was getting more and more nervous and was beginning to regret encouraging Topaz to enter the contest.

'Please welcome Octavia Quaver!' Bradley called out, and Octavia strutted on to the stage.

The audience gasped. Topaz groaned. Octavia looked like a star. Perched high on her head was a headdress made of pink feathers. A tight sequinned bodice ended just below her waist and then exploded into a skirt of pink net and feathers. She looked like a pink bird of paradise. Even Pauline was wearing a dress that matched the colour of Octavia's outfit. Pauline pressed a button on the keyboard, the music started and Octavia began to sing.

'My name is Octavia, I love to perform
It's great to be here now, I'll go down a storm . . .'

She had a voice like liquid honey. She sang, she shimmied, she batted her eyelashes and fluttered her feathers. The audience loved her.

Zelma Flint stopped sucking her pen and leant forward to get a closer look.

'Look at her!' Topaz whispered to Ruby. 'I can't compete with that!'

'Of course you can,' Ruby whispered back. 'You don't need all those feathers and stuff to show you have talent.'

Octavia came to the end of her act and the audience went wild. A beaming Pauline sat at the keyboard and clapped louder and faster than anyone else. Topaz wondered whether the fact that Pauline was so close to the clapometer would make any difference.

'It's a score of eleven o'clock!' shouted Bradley above the noise of the audience. 'Miss Octavia Quaver is in the lead!'

Clutching her handbag, Pauline Quaver rushed to the back of the stage and darted behind the curtain as Octavia smiled, waved, curtsied and practically had to be pushed off the stage by Bradley Bennett.

'And now for our next act, Topaz L'Amour and Ruby Ruddle, otherwise known as The Gem Set!'

'That's us!' said Topaz, grabbing Ruby's arm. 'We're on!'

They walked out on to the stage. She could see her mother and Sapphire in the audience. Pauline Quaver was racing back to her seat. The crowd, still excited at Octavia's performance, cheered loudly. As Ruby sat down at the keyboard, Topaz leant against it.

'Take it away, Ruby!' she called out, twirling her cane.

Ruby hit the first key but the only sound that came out was a dull *Phut!* Topaz kept her smile stretched across her face as Ruby tried again. *Phut!*

'The keyboard isn't working!' hissed Ruby, madly flicking switches and twiddling knobs.

Phut phut phut.

'It was working for Octavia!' Ruby sounded desperate.

Phut phut phut.

Standing in the wings, Bradley Bennett looked worried. Next to the Clapometer Clock, Poppy looked confused. The audience began to fidget and talk amongst themselves.

Bradley bounded on to the stage. 'Ladies and gentlemen, there's a slight technical problem for The Gem Set, but we're sorting it out.' He turned to Ruby. 'Is it plugged in?' he hissed.

Ruby darted behind the curtain and followed the lead of the keyboard to the wall. It wasn't just that the keyboard hadn't been plugged in. The plug was missing!

Ruby put her head around the curtain and showed Topaz the plug-less wire. She hadn't wanted to perform, but she didn't want to let Topaz down. Without a plug, the keyboard wouldn't play a note. *There wouldn't be this problem with a piano!* she thought.

Topaz stood in the spotlight and looked out at the audience, many of whom were so bored they had left their seats to get more drinks. People were talking amongst themselves. Zelma Flint was barking into her mobile phone and chewing her pen.

I'm here with a crumpled top hat, no music, and trainers studded with drawing-pins! thought Topaz. *Now what?*

But as she stood there, it took her back to the days before she was at Precious Gems, days when she spent hours practising dance moves in her bedroom, tap-dancing on the bathroom floor in her modified trainers and moving to music she'd heard on the radio. When she'd auditioned for Precious Gems she didn't have any music or fancy costumes or proper tap-shoes. The sheer thrill of performing had made Miss Diamond notice her and give her a place. The song and dance routine she'd perfected in her bedroom more than a year ago came flooding back. She tapped her cane on the floor, doffed her battered top hat and started to sing and dance. The noise of people talking began to fade. Those who had gone to the bar began to drift back towards their seats. Glasses stopped clinking. Children stopped crying. Zelma Flint put down her mobile phone. Everyone was mesmerized by the girl in the scruffy top hat and odd shoes who was lighting up the stage more brightly than any spotlight ever could.

With a final twirl of her cane and a flip of her hat, Topaz ended her routine.

I won't win, she thought. *But I've enjoyed every minute of being up here.*

The crowd went wild. The clapometer scale reached eleven o'clock. Bradley Bennett and Poppy beamed.

'Topaz L'Amour and Octavia Quaver are tying for first place!' shouted Bradley, as there was more clapping and cheering. 'Zelma Flint, stand by! We may need your vote!'

Topaz left the stage and bumped into a furious Octavia and Pauline. Octavia may have looked like a bird of paradise on stage, but she was squawking like a demented pink parrot off it.

'I demand a reclap!' she was screeching. 'I was the clear winner.'

'This is a fix!' yelled Pauline, looking as if she might explode with anger.

'It wasn't, but *you* tried to fix it,' Topaz's mother appeared. She had the same steely expression in her eyes as when she'd been angry with Topaz the day before.

'What do you mean?' demanded Pauline.

'We saw you come back to your seat with a

screwdriver sticking out of your handbag,' said Sapphire. '*You* removed the plug from the keyboard.'

'Mum!' whined Octavia. 'Don't let her speak to you like that.'

'We saw you,' said Lola calmly. 'Don't try to deny it!'

Pauline's face was like thunder. She thrust her bag towards Lola. 'How dare you accuse me! There's no screwdriver in my bag – look for yourself!' She tore open her handbag and flashed it towards Lola, too quickly for anyone to see whether there was a screwdriver, but just quickly enough for Topaz to notice a flash of sparkly red amongst the jumble of used tissues and empty sweet wrappers.

'The ribbons to my tap-shoes!' gasped Topaz. 'You've got the ribbons to my tap-shoes. You *did* steal them after all!'

'Oh, so what if we did?' snapped Pauline. 'Fat lot of good it's done us.'

'Zelma Flint is a rubbish agent,' whined a sour-faced Octavia, her feathers clearly ruffled in more ways than one. 'Even if she votes for me, I'd want a better agent than her.'

'I think we're all forgetting something,' said Ruby. 'Neither of you have won yet. There is still one more contestant, Candy Stripe and Honey.'

'Who?' said Topaz, Lola, Pauline and Octavia in unison.

'Her,' said Sapphire pointing towards the wings where a young girl, about three years of age, stood sobbing, clutching a pink and white teddy bear. She was dressed from head to toe in pink, with pink ribbons in her blonde hair. A woman stood over her, her hands on her hips and her face set in a snarl.

'Get on to that stage, Candy, or there'll be no chicken nuggets for you tonight!' she hissed.

'Don't want to!' Candy sobbed, sucking her thumb and burying her tear-stained face into her teddy.

'How dreadful to have such a pushy mother,' said Octavia as Candy's mother continued to order her daughter on stage and Candy refused to move.

Bradley Bennett popped backstage.

'Is Candy coming out?' he said in a slightly brittle voice. 'The timings for this show have gone haywire!'

'She's coming!' snapped Mrs Stripe, as with an almighty push she propelled Candy through the curtain and on to the stage where she stood looking bewildered under the spotlight, sucking her thumb with one hand and clutching her teddy, Honey, with the other.

'Ahhh . . .' the audience swooned.

Topaz noticed with some alarm that the clapometer

rose to a higher score without Candy even uttering a word than Trevor the lip-moving bushy-eyebrowed ventriloquist had managed during his entire act.

Bradley came across to Candy and crouched beside her, the sequins on his trousers crackling into the microphone.

'My name is Bradley. What are you going to sing for us, Candy?' he asked.

Candy said nothing but a voice from behind the curtain screeched, 'She's going to sing "Twinkle Twinkle Little Star"!'

Candy looked as if she'd like to run behind the curtain, if only her mother weren't behind it.

'Start with me,' said Bradley. 'Twinkle Twinkle Little Star, How I Wonder . . .'

In between sobs and thumb-sucking, Candy began to lisp the words to the song, occasionally stopping to wipe away a tear or give her teddy an extra hug. The audience seemed to be willing her to sing every note. If she stopped for more than a moment, her mother could be heard yelling the words from the wings.

Barely had Candy lisped the final note when the audience went wild, the clapometer needle shot up to eleven o'clock, then twelve o'clock and then tried to go round again before there was a *Boing!*, a snapping noise and the needle fell to the floor, landing on Bradley Bennett's foot.

'I think we can safely say we have a winner!' announced Bradley, hopping around trying to rub his foot and smile at the same time. 'Candy Stripe and Honey!'

Candy's mum ran on stage and grabbed the envelope off Zelma Flint who had come up for the prize giving. 'Can you make my daughter a star?' Mrs Stripe demanded.

'I'm having this place under trade descriptions!' yelled Pauline Quaver as Octavia sobbed into her feathers. 'It's billed as a talent show and that terrible tot has no talent! She got the sympathy vote!'

Sapphire and Ruby hugged Topaz. 'You must be very disappointed,' said Sapphire. 'I know how much you wanted to win.'

'At least Octavia didn't win either,' said Ruby.

Topaz looked across at Octavia who was sobbing and wiping her nose with a handful of feathers.

'Oh, show business isn't always about talent, but about what the audience wants. I don't mind.'

Ruby and Sapphire looked at their friend in amazement. *That's something we never thought we'd hear Topaz say*, they thought.

'Did you have a nice time?' Rodney Ruddle hugged his daughter as he met her off the train.

'Fantastic!' said Ruby. 'What about you?'

'Terrible,' replied her father. 'We didn't see a single

Bolascan slug. It was baking hot so they didn't come out to mate. It's always wet there at this time of year. We're blaming it on global warming.'

'Mum!' exclaimed Sapphire, astonished to see her mother, accompanied by Rupert and Parks. 'What are you doing here? I thought you'd still be sunbathing on the tropical island.'

Vanessa Stratton shuddered. 'I came home early. The weather was simply dreadful. It's always baking at this time of year, but it rained non-stop, all day, every day. The humidity played havoc with my hair. I'm blaming it on global warming. Did you have a lovely time?'

'Brilliant!' said Sapphire.

Topaz watched her friends disappear into the distance and back to their own lives. She'd see them in the holidays and they'd ring each other, but it wasn't like being at school every day.

'Thanks for a fantastic holiday, Mum,' said Topaz as she watched a bad-tempered Octavia and her mother struggle down the platform with their bags.

Lola put her arm round her daughter's shoulders.

'Now,' she said. 'You've got the rest of the holidays to enjoy before you get down to schoolwork, and make sure the next report you get doesn't need to be hidden.'

Topaz nodded. 'I know! I can't wait for next term.'

Now that's something I never thought I'd hear Topaz say, thought Lola.

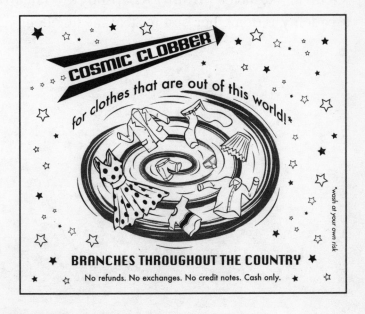

Another sparkling Topaz production!

Topaz Steals the Show
by Helen Bailey

Topaz L'Amour is ecstatic – she's won a place at Precious Gems Stage School! But in the world of show business, learning to tap dance on the bathroom floor with drawing pins in your trainers counts for nothing. Topaz quickly learns that life at stage school is hard work.

And she doesn't just have to cope with lack of training. Her rival, the scheming and ambitious Octavia Quaver from Rhapsody's Theatre Academy, is doing her best to steal the limelight . . .